THE S

MASTE

VANESSA BROOKS

Published by Blushing Books®,
a subsidiary of
ABCD Graphics and Design
977 Seminole Trail #233
Charlottesville, VA 22901
The trademark Blushing Books®
is registered in the US Patent and Trademark Office.

Vanessa Brooks
The Smuggler's Bride

EBook ISBN: 978-1-61258-528-4
Print ISBN: 978-1-61258-571-0

Cover Art by ABCD Graphics & Design

GLOSSARY OF CORNISH WORDS USED IN THIS TALE

Kara = love
Keresik = darling
Party = young woman
Toll-din = arsehole
Melder = sweetheart or darling
Heller = naughty, ill-behaved youngster.
Henting = raining hard
Gisson = talking rubbish
Kyjya = fuck
Sug ow halgh = suck my dick
Avynn'ta ow dogluthi? = d'you want me to fuck you?

CHAPTER 1

Primrose Latimer stared dismally at the tiny puddle growing between her hands, which were placed flat upon the wood-planked floor of a ship's cabin. Her tears continued to track downward, relentlessly swelling the small saline pool. She recognised her own folly, berating herself for her impetuous behaviour. She fully understood she would not be in her present ignominious predicament, face down, pressed snugly over a smuggler's hard thigh, if only she had practiced a modicum of common sense. Unfortunately, using rationale and controlling her volatile temper was not one of her finer points. The devil landed another heavy thwack upon her tender rump, chuckling fiendishly as the blow shifted her forward so that her elbows locked and her hands braced against the rough floor. She'd been naïve to think the bastard wouldn't carry out his evil threat to spank her but for some reason she'd honestly believed he was bluffing, probably because no man had ever dared to lay a hand in discipline upon her genteel person before.

Another strike fell, causing her to wail. She shifted, swaying her rounded derriere in an attempt to escape the brute's retribution. What on earth had possessed her to whack his smugly arrogant face? She faced the fact that it was because he'd had the audacity to laugh at her feeble attempts to evade capture. There it was again, that deep resonating laugh, the sound so utterly arrogant. She ground her teeth; the buccaneer was deriving far too much enjoyment from her embarrassing position. "I shall enjoy watching you choke when you dance at the end of a rope, you *filthy* blaggard!" she snarled, squealing when his response landed with searing accuracy across her upper thighs. Punishing smacks continued to rain down upon the delicate pale flesh of her upper legs, silencing her. The shock of the scalding slaps caused so much pain that in her distress, she wept.

"I might be a blaggard but I strongly object to being called filthy. Unlike most men, I bathe daily, more oft than not in the ocean. As to your pleasure should I end up dangling from a gibbet, I confess myself to be singularly unsurprised to hear that, because you are without doubt one of the nastiest pieces of skirt it has been my misfortune to meet. Your milksop fiancé is welcome to you, however much I pity the poor *toll-din,* especially since he sounds like such a popinjay. I suspect he will never have the bollocks to thrash you as thoroughly as your peevish tongue deserves!"

Primrose's response to this scathing description of her intended resonated clearly about the ship: she shrieked her furious anger and frustration. The knave chuckled; it was obvious to her that he was deriving too much gratification from the spanking.

Pasco had dumped her upon deck earlier and tugged off the sack covering her head, revealing the unexpected, a young woman with riotous pale ringlets cascading down her back. Jago had been confounded to see not fear in her overlarge, baby blue eyes, but fury. Even when she'd cast her haughty gaze over his motley crew, most of whom were armed to the teeth, gathered about her with obvious lewd interest, she'd lifted her chin and spat in the bosun's eye. As she screamed abuse at her captors, her courage had him intrigued. Studying the haughty beauty, Jago Poldrunne found himself admiring her spirit.

"Well there's a surprise, Pasco, you've managed to capture a mermaid. Where is the older lady you were actually sent to fetch?"

"*Kyjya*!" Pasco swore in his native Cornish. Shocked, he'd spun a half circle, pushed his face into hers and asked, "Who the devil d'you be?"

Shaking her dishevelled tresses back from her face, the bint straightened her back, proudly declaring herself to be Miss Primrose Latimer of Caulderstone House, Surrey, before bravely—or foolishly—demanding to know who they were, so that upon her return ashore she could inform the Excise men. Bending and untying her ankles, she'd stalked over to the gangplank and hopped up onto the ramp, obviously resolved to leave. Jago immediately demanded her return but she deliberately ignored him and his subsequent threat to spank her if she dared to disobey. Before Primrose knew what he was about, he'd strode across the deck, scooped her up and thrown her over his shoulder, bellowing the order to set sail.

As soon as he'd lowered her to the deck, grinning at her feeble struggles, she'd struck him across the chin with a fid, garnered from the deck. The damned things were everywhere since they were used daily to splice rope. His face brutalised, he'd flung her back over his shoulder. No amount of kicking and screaming deterred Jago from his single minded purpose. She'd shrieked her rage, kicking her dainty stockinged feet, but made no headway against his formidable strength. His crew guffawed gleefully as their captain landed a meaty thwack upon her delectable arse, causing her to caterwaul like a banshee.

So here they were, ensconced together within his cabin. He in his captain's chair with her tossed cosily across his lap, doing her utmost to avoid his correcting palm with absolutely no success. Strangely, Jago could not remember the last time he'd enjoyed himself quite so much. She might be a scold but the lass had courage, he'd give her that. She was a comely baggage, albeit one with a sharp tongue. Although she deigned to show no fear, he had to admire her courage in what must be a singularly frightening situation for her. He continued to raise his arm, bringing it down with strong emphasis, until she slumped dejectedly across his knee. Only then did he lower his hand to rest upon her rounded posterior. Gently he massaged her heated globes, and she moaned, unconsciously shifting her hips upward to meet his soothing palm.

"Are you going to make me walk the plank?" she asked tremulously.

He detected the trepidation in her voice and grinned. "Nay, we are neither pirates nor wreckers, my mermaid," he reassured.

"I am not *'your'* anything. My name is Miss Primrose Latimer, why do you insist on calling me by that ridiculous name!" Her tone was razor sharp. He sighed, landing another warning thwack upon her delectable arse. She shrieked more with rage than pain.

"You are as far removed from a primrose as you could possibly be. A mermaid is a wicked siren; the title suits you rather well. I need to decide what to do with you. For now, I intend locking you in my cabin while I go and take stock." He swung her up onto his lap, coming face to face with blue eyes sheened with tears. He made no attempt to comfort her. "Learn to do as you're told then we might deal well enough together. Defy me and your backside shall pay the price. Now be a good little shrew while I am gone, try not to break anything. In fact, for every broken object I find on my return, you shall receive ten licks of my razor strop."

He scooped her up and walked over to the box bed, where he dumped her unceremoniously from waist height. She squealed as she landed, Jago wasn't sure whether from rage or pain since she'd landed on her arse. "*You*... you filthy turd!" she swore, shrilly.

He swiftly grasped her chin, forcing her face up, bending so his nose was an inch from hers. "If you keep up your foul language I shall be forced to silence you. I doubt your Timothy has shoved his cock between those bee-stung lips of yorn. Be advised that I have no such inhibitions about teaching you what a woman's mouth is truly designed for! I suggest you have a care, my mermaid!" He cast aside her quivering chin and stalked out of the cabin.

Primrose found herself alone. She gaped as his filthy suggestion sank into her shocked mind. Did men really do such things with women? Surely he was jesting? By the time her wits were restored enough to ask him, he'd gone, the key turned in the lock. She clambered off the bed, bemused and not a little irritated by his comment. Crossly she wandered about the cabin, absentmindedly rubbing her chastised behind whilst perusing the room. It was tidy except for some papers littering the heavy wooden desk. On a table, charts were laid out, along with an odd-looking scientific instrument, perhaps some kind of sextant. A heavy glass inkwell sat weighting down an open scroll. Without giving the matter much consideration, she picked up the blue glass liner from inside the inkwell then dribbled ink right across the parchment. Espying an unopened tin, she rattled it. Tugging the lid free she discovered that it held hobnails. A pair of fashionable leather, high-topped boots, leant drunkenly against a large clothing chest. Wandering over to them, opening the top of one smart boot, she tilted the tin, watching with satisfaction as half the nails disappeared into the dark recess of the boot. She repeated her malicious act with the other. Turning to replace the tin, she noticed the cabin had a small, dingy port-hole window. Launching the empty tin carelessly back onto the desk, she hurried over to examine the rounded structure, which appeared to open outwards with the aid of a top hinge.

Musing over the width of the gap, she disrobed, knowing that she could never fit through the gap wearing her bulky gown. Dressed only in her chemise, she thought she might stand a chance of escape. Leaning out, she gazed down at the churning sea below. It was a long way down but unlike many other ladies of her class, Primrose Latimer could swim. Her father Christopher had taught her, in the lake situated in the grounds at Caulderstone House.

A ledge ran along the side of the ship, one large enough for her toes to grip and her to balance on. If she could lower herself onto that ridge, she might be able to edge her way along and perhaps find another way inside the ship, thus enabling her to hide until they reached shore, where she could make good her escape. Levering herself up onto the rounded window ledge she pushed her arms through, then her shoulders before realising that this wouldn't do at all. Maybe she needed to go out feet first? So intent was she on her escape that the sudden slap to her bottom caused her to start violently.

"It was good of you to present yourself ready for punishment. I see a day of hard work has been wasted by your petty revenge; pouring ink all over my charts." He shook his head sadly. "Such a stupid thing to do! How d'you think a ship is navigated, eh? I conclude the destruction you wrought as breakage. I tally ten stripes of my razor strop."

Primrose struggled to push back inside the cabin but the material covering her bosom seemed to be caught on a hook under the wooden ledge. She cursed, panicking as the fabric ripped. She was about to launch herself backward when a large hand was placed in the small of her back, holding her firmly in place. Her bottom and legs were inside, while her head and shoulders were out. Without prior warning, a line of fire streaked across her backside.

Primrose reared up so fast she smacked the back of her head on the porthole frame, hollering loudly at the painful blow. "Stay downward, you foolish bint," the devil ordered, without pity for her demise.

Primrose sobbed as her rear end was roasted, scalded with powerful thwacks from his leather strap, an object that felt as though it had teeth that were biting and branding her shrivelling flesh. It was a dreadful punishment, causing her to quake as every singeing line of fire burned deep into her girlish rounded nates. The chastisement overwhelmed her; she screamed her distress into the sea breeze where her raucous cries were lost, dispersed by the salty gusts, which rendered her shrieks as insubstantial as sea vapour.

A hand clasped her head, protecting it from another knock against the frame as she was hauled backwards into the cabin. She turned her tear-drenched face toward her captor and tormentor, surprised to see a look of lascivious surprise upon his face. "Cover yourself!" he barked. She glanced down to see the torn material of her chemise, her breasts spilled free, bare to his gaze.

Placing a hand strategically to cover her bosom, she glared at him. "With what, pray? You are responsible for this!" Her hand gestured down her body.

The fiend gave a strangled growl and spun away, presenting his back to her. "Dress yourself!" he commanded. Ignoring him, Primrose cast herself face down upon the bed, burying her face into the bed clothes. She beat her fists and wept. Her bottom hurt beyond anything she'd ever experienced before. Totally overwrought, she sobbed pitifully into the pillows, barely noticing when he slammed out of the cabin.

"WHAT DO 'EE DO NOW? We needed t' Lord's wife to force the bastard to pay us what 'ee owes. We canna float about the channel with a hold full o' *Cousin Jackie* for verra long, not with the Excise men combing the waters for us an' those damned wreckers day an' night!"

Jago pinched the bridge of his nose. "Tell me something I don't know, Pasco. I'll sleep on it for now. I'll reveal my plan in the morning." He'd been quick to learn that if he was to maintain control of the rough seamen who manned the *Mermaid's Tail,* he needed to maintain leadership, never showing indecisiveness. It would not do to share the fact that he'd no clue as to his next move. Hopefully, by morning, he would have a plan but if not, well, he would cobble something together to keep them all safe from the hangman's noose.

They'd flitted back and forth across the Channel with no problems other than the vagaries of the weather for the past year, fetching good brandy and spices such as the heavily taxed pepper back to Cornwall, where rich and poor alike bought quantities of the colloquially labelled *'Cousin Jackie',* at an inflated price. Their goods were still cheaper than the taxed goods brought into the country under the usual legal trade route. It made a good living for those cast out from the foreclosed tin mines which could no longer match the cheaper imports from Australia and South Africa. All had gone well until recently, when their best paying patron took it into his head to blackmail Jago and his men. This greedy Lordship wanted in on their operation. He'd threatened to tell the Excise men about their illegal activities unless they cut him a share of the profits. The fact that Jago was squire and would go free while his friends perished was enough to force his hand against his greedy patron. Jago determined drastic measures.

The plan to kidnap his Lordship's wife in order to convince her of their just cause and thus enlist her help had sorely backfired. Now they were stuck with a ship full of illegal contraband, nowhere to stow it, and an unknown but shrewish *pretty* who seemed to want to see the lot of them strung up on a gibbet.

Their home port was well hidden, three inlets down from Porthcollen Bay, the sandy cove screened from plain sight by high cliffs which hid the schooner as it slid in and out of the inlet with easy discretion. The cave and passage that led up to the house, set high above the sea, remained undiscovered. Unfortunately it was at present full to bursting with barrels of contraband. There was nowhere to offload their cargo, especially now that their titled customer decided he had no intention of paying for his goods.

Jago pondered upon the girl locked in his cabin with growing unease He was not inclined to regret; the woman had behaved atrociously, she'd brought this misery upon herself. She was a comely enough wench; he'd had to stifle his reaction at the sight of her soft, white, rosy tipped breasts softly beckoning to him from across the floor. They begged to be fondled, their puckered peaks teasing, or was that simply his cock talking? Silver tongued, demanding that he introduce him to their pillowing solace? He shook his head to silence the insidious voice of one that had been ignored too long.

The question was what to do with the chit? He baulked at the two choices laid before him, neither held any allure. Kill the woman or, God forbid, marry her, each choice seeming as bad as the other. She needed to be silenced but for the life of him he couldn't think of another way to ensure her mouth remained shut. Cut out her tongue? He gave a rueful chuckle, he was no pirate. He couldn't murder—pillage, hmm, perhaps—but kill in cold blood? No, never, not him. He was no wrecker, should he find the men responsible for the luring of cargo ships onto Cornish rocks, well then yes, he'd happily cut those evil bastard's throats.

If only the girl was a timid lass, one he could scare into silence, but this termagant? Hell, she'd have Excise men breathing down their necks the moment she set foot ashore, the vixen. Sarding hell, as far as he could see, he'd no choice other than to marry the woman, simply to ensure her silence. Since the law stated a wife could not testify against her husband, that would perhaps be his best course of action. By Gad, he needed a drink; the hold was full of *Cousin Jackie,* so why not? Jago felt he'd earned a bottle of his own contraband.

~

BACK INSIDE THE captain's cabin, Primrose was done weeping. Enraged, she determined to continue with her original plan of escape. In desperation she stripped off all her clothes, every last stitch, until she stood nude. Quickly winding her long fair hair into a pony tail, she knotted it high atop her head. Standing on a chair, she wriggled and squeezed her flesh through the porthole, inching forward painfully, in no doubt that she would suffer bruising as she edged her way out of the cabin. Her arms braced against the ship's side in order to hold herself away from the wooden structure. If the scraping soreness along her spine was any indication, she'd suffer some nasty abrasions across her back but she had to get away before that bastard returned to finish her off. Primrose could see no other way for this to end well for her. The smugglers wouldn't let her go because they knew full well she'd bring the authorities crashing down upon their evil heads; therefore the only way to silence her would be to kill her. No one was coming to her rescue, it was up to her to save herself, and dammit, she would!

Ignoring the sickening distance to the churning ocean below, Primrose wriggled and twisted until at last she felt the dizzying sensation of free fall. She dropped from the porthole down into the dark waters below. Her shoulder cracked painfully against the side of the ship as she fell, then black waters closed freezingly over her head. Spluttering, she bobbed to the surface and began to swim frantically away from the slow moving ship. It was shocking how quickly the schooner left her behind. Teeth chattering violently from cold, she glanced about her, treading water. Thank goodness Papa had the foresight to teach her to swim. A single pale glow indicated that land may lie to her right, the light from a house along the shore perhaps? She struck out in that direction, fighting against strong swells and currents that felt as though they wanted to drag her further out to sea.

~

JAGO STARED at the empty cabin in disbelief. Gone! How the devil had she managed to get through that tiny porthole? He bent down and retrieved her clothing. Shaking his head, he realised that she must have gone into the sea stark naked. Perhaps she'd been a mermaid after all? He dashed to the opening and struck his head out but could see nothing. Turning, he flew out of the door, shouting orders to the helmsman to steer the ship full circle port but ordering him to come about slow; concerned that in turning they might strike the girl.

"What's the problem?" Pasco asked, striding toward him.

"The woman, she's thrown herself overboard!"

Pasco grabbed his arm, yanking him around so they were face to face. "Then leave her be. Let Davy Jones do our work for us!" he growled.

Jago shrugged the man free, glaring at him with disgust. "I am no murderer of innocents, nor are you, Pasco, you have a wife and daughter, man. I cannot believe you'd wish any woman to die in such a way!"

"Think on it, Poldrunne, no wench of her class can swim. She'll last mere moments out there in the swell. Let her go, Jago, she made her choice, you didn't ask her to jump. She's made it easy for us! Come, have a taste o'*jackie* an' accept that she's gone."

Jago ignored the man completely and shouted for lanterns to be brought, ordering his men to hang over the ship's side, lighting as much of the sea below as they could. He ordered a boat lowered with a crew of two, who rowed around the starboard side first, searching for the missing woman.

After an hour, Jago admitted defeat. There was no sign of the girl. He recalled his men, setting a course for Porthcothon and home. He slammed into his cabin with a bottle of good *Jackie* and lay on his bunk. Her bundle of clothing lay upon the floor; he reached over and clasped her under garments to his chest. A faint smell of citrus fruit emanated from the soft material. He lowered his nose and buried his face into her garments, recalling her pretty face.

Marriage to the wench now seemed, in retrospect, to be a happier option. He took another swig from the thick brown bottle; liquid gold warmed his throat as he absently rubbed the ache in his bruised chinbone. Jago prayed that he could drink enough to dull his conscience sufficiently to sleep but somehow he doubted oblivion would be his. He tipped and drank repetitively, his heart heavy with remorse.

CHAPTER 2

Primrose gradually became aware of voices whispering nearby, but she failed to identify any of the words spoken since they appeared to be talking in another tongue. A glass was held to her lips, her head lifted so she could drink from the proffered vessel. Opening her eyes, she looked into the pale rheumy eyes of a swarthy peasant woman dressed in the cap and apron of a servant. It appeared she was inside a lowly dwelling. Smiling toothlessly down at Primrose, the woman encouraged her to drink. She sipped gratefully, the sweet liquid slipping easily down her parched throat. Her vulgar stomach chose that moment to remind her and those close by that she hadn't eaten recently. This prompted the woman beside her to pick up a wooden bowl and spoon, which she offered to Primrose. Attempting to sit, she slumped back when the room began to spin. Clutching her aching head, she took a moment to recover before gratefully reaching for the bowl. Tasting the dish, she discovered it to be an aromatic rabbit stew. "Delicious!" she exclaimed politely, then tucked in ravenously. The old woman wagged her head with approval.

Once finished, Primrose thanked her hostess, asking if she spoke English.

"Aye, o'course."

Primrose sighed with relief. "I need to find Lady Trewithe; she is my intended's aunt-in-law. I am staying with the family at Pencullen House but, unbelievably, I was kidnapped by smugglers. Can you send word to Pencullen that I am here?"

The woman nodded. "Aye mistress, but t'would be just as easy for Sam to take 'ee in t' cart." She nodded across the room to where a younger, tow-haired, solidly built young man sat staring fixedly at her. "T'was my son Sam as found 'ee on t'shore. He thought 'ee was a dead mermaid! Right disappointed 'ee was when 'ee saw thy legs an' no fish tail a 'laying in t' surf. T'were lucky t'was summer, otherwise t' sea would have been so cold t'would like have perished."

Primrose barely understood her heavy lilting accent. She focused on the fact the woman mentioned that they owned a conveyance. "You have a cart, you say?"

The old woman cocked her head sideways, grinning. "Oh aye."

Primrose smiled, nodding to show she'd understood. As soon as she began to toss back the thin blanket that covered her, she realised that she was stark naked underneath. Blushing, she gestured down the length of her body. The woman appeared to understand. She moved across the room to where a plain wooden chest stood. Lifting the lid, muttering to herself, she rummaged about inside, finally pulling forth a drab grey gown.

Primrose didn't much like the way the man, Sam, stared. She waved him away but he either didn't understand her gesticulation or he didn't want to leave the room while she pulled on the wretched garment. Huffily she dressed with difficulty beneath the ragged blanket. Her bones and muscles ached as she shifted to and fro in an attempt to pull the dress discreetly down over her body, noticing a mass of abrasions covering her limbs. Once dressed, she hopped up from the cot bed. Immediately the room swam and she flung out an arm to steady herself, pausing until the nausea passed before taking up the threadbare blanket to wrap about herself for warmth. Shivering violently, she wondered whether she was suffering a fever. She needed to return to Pencullen to seek help—and quickly.

"I shall repay your kindness generously with coin once I am safely delivered to Pencullen House. I thank you, good woman; you and your son have saved my life. A debt I promise I'll not soon forget. Apply to me if ever you find yourself in need of assistance."

Sam stood; silently he led her from the dark cottage. As Primrose passed by, the old woman caught the edge of her blanket. "I be Kerra Tucket," she told her. Primrose held out her hand to the woman who lifted her palm, yet hesitated.

Primrose grasped her hand firmly in her own, covering it with her palm. "I am Primrose Latimer, Kerra. I am pleased to make your acquaintance."

The old woman smiled and nodded. Primrose bent on impulse, she kissed Kerra's sunken cheek. "Thee 'ave a need 'o me, I be here. Go, an' God speed, lass!" She gave Primrose a gentle shove toward her son, seated atop a basic wooden cart, to which a sway backed old nag was hitched. Primrose turned as they drove away from the cottage, she lifted her hand in farewell.

Kerra watched them go without returning the friendly gesture. She remained stationary, huddled under the stoop of the ancient cottage doorframe. Her gift of second sight flooded her senses. From the moment she'd touched the girl's hand, she'd felt the connection. Her head wagged with deep and knowing satisfaction. Her appearance was meant to be.

Twice Primrose drifted into an uncomfortable doze, only to be awoken by the lurching of the wooden cart as it thumped in and out of the ruts and grooves of the rough dirt track. It was dusk before they entered the imposing ironwork gates of Pencullen, and some fifteen minutes more before the twisted chimneys of the grey stone house came into view. Sam began to head for the tradesmen's entrance at the back of the mansion but Primrose placed her hand on his arm, commanding him to pull around to the front steps. Sam helped her down. Primrose tried to bring order to her salty, sand filled locks. Her knees suddenly buckled under her, Sam picked her up, he tossed her over his shoulder like a sack of coal and carried her up to the imposing entrance of the house. He pulled the iron handle that jangled a bell somewhere deep within the recess of the house.

The door was finally opened by a butler, who raked a disdainful eye over the poorly dressed duo who'd dared to come to the front door of Pencullen.

"Darrent, it is Miss Latimer," Primrose told him wearily. "Do you recall that I am staying as a guest here?" The butler opened the door wide enough to allow Sam to step through, whereupon he hauled his burden across the spacious entrance and deposited Primrose into a wooden, hall chair. "Thank you, Sam." Primrose held out her arm, offering her hand to the lad. He stared at it then glanced at Primrose's face as if suspecting a trap. "Thank you," she encouraged softly. Hesitating, he put out his large dirty hand, and she shook it. Awkwardly he turned and lumbered outside without a backward glance. "Wait! Sam, wait!" Primrose cried but he didn't appear to hear her reedy cry. "I need to give him coin!" she wailed.

"Tucket!" Darrent bellowed commandingly. Sam stopped; he swung around, glowering at the butler. "Here, take this, the lady wishes you to have it." He held out some coin, taken from his own pocket. Sam moved back into the entrance and, after taking the proffered money, he tugged his forelock, turned and stomped away. The butler closed the door.

"Why thank you, Darrent, I shall recompense you as soon as may be."

The butler inclined his head. "Thank you, Miss Latimer. Your absence has caused uproar within the house. His Lordship and my Lady Trewithe will certainly be glad to see you safely delivered. Please wait here while I inform them of your return." Darrent sounded bland as he moved away at his usual stately pace leaving

Primrose swaying in her chair, feeling light-headed and extremely chilled.

"My dear child! My goodness wherever have you been, *whatever are you wearing*? Quick, Darrent, the poor girl is swooning! Quickly now, and fetch a footman to carry her up to her chamber. Oh, and order a warming pan to heat her bed. Come along, quickly, snap, snap, the gal is failing fast!"

When Primrose once again became conscious of her surroundings, it was a relief to find that on this occasion she was settled comfortably between clean sheets, snuggled into a warm bed, tended by a maid. She yawned mightily and stretched, wincing as her aching muscles protested. Memories of her abduction flooded back, and she attempted to sit only to groan aloud as she slumped back against the pillows, her body throbbing complainingly from the sudden movement.

The maid rushed to the bell pull and yanked hard upon the cord. "Stay still, miss, you mustn't move about so! I am ordered to summon the doctor and Lady Trewithe once you awoke."

Primrose rested drowsily as instructed. She made no attempt to move, for it hurt too much.

The doctor arrived, followed by an agitated Lady Trewithe. She immediately went to Primrose's bedside. Bending to kiss her forehead, she chattered. "You have no idea of the worry you have caused us, dear child! I am so happy to see you awake at last and looking really quite well… Is she well, Doctor?" she spun to ask a grey haired and bearded man, who had, in deference to his patron, allowed her to approach Primrose first.

"I shall need to examine the young lady before I can make a diagnosis, your Ladyship."

"Of course, yes, of course!" Lady Trewithe stood back to make way for the doctor, who moved to Primrose's side. He lifted his pocket watch from inside his waistcoat and taking her wrist into his opposite hand, he studied the watch. "How do you feel, Miss

Latimer?" he asked as he laid her hand back down onto the counterpane.

"I ache everywhere!" she complained.

"I am not at all surprised to hear that. I need to examine you, please roll onto your front, my dear." He pulled up her nightgown and clicked his tongue. Reaching into his bag he produced a jar of salve which he proceeded to smear over her back and flanks. "You have extensive bruising all across your person, and minor lacerations which I have treated with a medicinal salve. Your afflictions should heal given time. You are a very lucky young woman to be in such rude health, many would have died from the chills you have suffered. I wish to listen to your chest now, for which I shall need you to sit and lean forward. I am afraid it will cause you some discomfort but I do need to listen through your back to ascertain that your lungs are clear of fluid. I shall require a maid to assist me."

Between the two they lifted Primrose into a sitting position, bending her forward across a pillow given to support her ribs. He examined her amidst her groans but after he had placed his trumpet against her back and listened for a few moments, he pronounced her fit. He prescribed powders for her pain and ordered another twenty-four hours of bed rest before she attempted to join the household. He stated confidently that she would soon heal.

Once her visitors had left, Primrose enjoyed a dish of cool sweet flummery, fed to her by the maid. She was persuaded to take a draught of powders the doctor had left for her, sleeping undisturbed right through the night until the following morning.

"DID YOU ENJOY YOUR BATH, m'dear?"

Primrose sank into an accomplished curtsy before the master of the house. "I did, my Lord, thank you. It felt good to wash away the salt and gritty sand from my hair."

Peter Trewithe gestured for her to be seated next to his wife, Verity. She greeted her young guest with a dimpled smile as she leant in to kiss Primrose's cheek.

"Do you feel well enough to share fully the tale of your unpleasant adventures?" he asked. Primrose nodded. "You may begin by explaining why you left the carriage when my wife asked you to remain inside and await her return." His reproach was clear.

Primrose automatically lifted her thumb to her mouth and bit down on her nail. Catching sight of the look of distaste on her host's face, she quickly lowered her hand to her lap. "Seconds after Lady Trewithe departed to visit the haberdashers, a man leapt into the carriage. He stuffed a rag into my mouth and threw a sack over my head before trussing me up with rope. He lifted me out of the carriage like a sack of potatoes. I felt myself flung face down over the pommel of a horse; we rode for short time while held in this uncomfortable position. Later I was lifted down from the horse and carried aboard the deck of a ship, the sack was removed and smugglers surrounded me, seemingly shocked to find that I was not another woman."

Primrose noticed husband and wife pass a significant glance between one another before Verity Trewithe exclaimed loudly, "Oh my dear, how simply terrifying… What an ordeal for you to suffer!" Lady Trewithe's hand fluttered nervously about her throat. It was the second time Primrose had been asked to repeat her sorry tale since she had been deemed well enough to join the household, although she had not yet had the opportunity to speak of it in front of Lord Trewithe. Until now she had not revealed the whole version of events—even now, she censored her sorry little tale. Up until this point, no one in the house had given reply to her own pressing question.

"Please, Lady Trewithe, I *beg* you answer me, regarding my Timothy, *where is he?*"

The lady exchanged a glance with her husband, who shrugged. She sighed. "I am sorry Miss Latimer, Primrose, there is no easy way for me to soften the blow. He returned to London. He has left you a missive, explaining the, er, situation… Would you, my dear?" She gestured to Lord Trewithe, who rose at once and went to a bureau where he extracted a parchment from a drawer to hand to his wife; she in turn passed it to Primrose.

"I think it best that I leave you two ladies alone for a little while. Miss Latimer, m'dear?" Lord Trewithe bowed to each woman in turn before hastily exiting the withdrawing room. He abhorred female hysterics. Since he knew full well what the letter contained, he had no doubt the contents would cause a more than usual dose of hysteria.

Meanwhile, Primrose broke the seal and began subconsciously chewing on her thumbnail as she read. Her face became ashen as the significance of the hateful letter sank in: Timothy wrote that he was breaking off their engagement.

Primrose had been insufferably pleased to be one of the first young ladies to become affianced during her London season. She had even teased a rival debutant about her lack of beau, only to discover the wretched girl already had a handsome secret admirer, Colonel French, to whom she was now long wedded. Primrose was engaged long before Claudia Weston, yet the hoyden had married within two months of meeting her beau. Sadly Primrose was back at square one, with no beau or fiancé. She would be a laughing stock back in Surrey and London, her reputation in tatters, all thanks to Timothy, who stated that he would not marry a woman who had been out alone and unescorted overnight. As far as he was concerned, she was disgraced.

"Can I not sue for breach of promise, my Lady?" she asked hopefully.

"I fear not, my dear. You were gone overnight; an event witnessed by the entire household. Timothy would simply call the servants as witnesses to your disappearance. Any judge worth his salt would rule that you were compromised. No man could be expected to keep his promise if there was the slightest hint that his fiancée had lain with another, perhaps even conceiving a child. No, I am sorry to say that you must face the fact that you are ruined, my dear, harsh as that may be."

Primrose dropped her head into her hands and moaned. "What of my word? I could swear on the Holy Bible that I was still pure!"

Lady Trewithe placed her hand over her young guest's comfortingly. "You know that it would not suffice. Another blow I have yet to share with you is the loss of your maid: Cox. It seems that she has become somewhat enamoured with Timothy's valet. I am sorry to say that she opted to return with them. Do not despair, I shall loan you the aid of a maid whenever you require. I actually have a suggestion to solve your other predicament too—that is, if you'd care to hear me out?"

Primrose looked at Lady Trewithe with sudden hope.

"No, no, I do not mean a solution with regards to Timothy. Ponsomby is far too morally fastidious to take you back after such an escapade. No, sadly you are ruined to him and to any others who will think alike. I am sorry to be so blunt but society is harsh to those who do not conform to the rules. No, I mean to suggest another match; one that I can almost guarantee. A liaison contracted with my own nephew, my sister Rowena's son. I am certain he will take you to wife."

Primrose frowned. "Why, what is wrong with him?" she asked suspiciously.

Lady Trewithe gave a tinkling laugh. "Nothing at all, I do assure you! James is a strapping, handsome young fellow, but a man who has no time for society frippery. You may find him a little, hmm, rough around the edges? Nonetheless he is a gentleman, the Squire of Poldrunne Manor no less! Admittedly, the house could use a woman's touch since his mother, my sister Rowena, died giving him birth. His father James died but two years ago. He slipped and fell down on icy steps and broke his back, poor fellow. T'was a terrible time for us all, it took six months of agony before the good Lord took the poor devil. So my nephew James has had little time for courtship but he tells me that he is ready to take a wife and breed in order to continue the family name."

Primrose was suspicious. Why was such a well connected lady of high birth, a member of Timothy's own family no less, so keen to help *her?* Perhaps her best course of action was to return to Caulderstone House in Surrey—and her parents. She cringed as she thought about her father's approbation. He would certainly be furious with her, even though none of the situation was her fault. Like most men, her father would not care about the whys and wherefores but only about the fact that she was ruined. It was general knowledge that no girl in society could be trusted not to be ruined when out alone for as long as she had been. It was unfair but then, London high society and members of the *haute ton* were cruel. Primrose knew that she, too, had been just as mean.

She remembered the various taunts and vicious snide remarks she'd made about other girls her age, many of whom she'd called friend. Perhaps remaining here, buried in Cornwall, far away from society gossip was for the best? After all, she would still be marrying into the renowned Trewithe family, albeit with a nephew on the maternal side as opposed to the paternal. Lady Trewithe must have noticed Primrose wavering because she interrupted her train of thought with a light tap on the arm with her closed fan.

"Come, child, let me organise a simple social occasion, just so you may cast an eye over him. See how you interact then decide what you think of the gentleman. Where's the harm in that, eh?"

Primrose had to agree. Her hostess was right, what harm could it do to meet the fellow? She was certainly out of matrimonial options, ruined as she was in the eyes of polite society.

CHAPTER 3

Primrose spent the next few days recuperating from her injuries. Her sore bottom was a discomfort she kept entirely to herself, although her long sojourn in the cold sea had assuaged most of the swelling to her punished backside. She still suffered twinges when she sat down thoughtlessly. She'd bitten her thumbnail almost to the quick, a habit she had broken aged ten but which she still resorted to now and then when stressed. Lord Trewithe persuaded her to write to her parents, explaining the situation, while his lady wife added a postscript to her letter in which she invited the Latimers to come and stay at Pencullen for a time, in order for the gossip to die down and let things settle.

The first morning that Primrose awoke finally pain free turned out to be dull, misty and uninspiring. Nevertheless, she ordered a horse to be prepared to take her riding after breakfast. She ate alone in the massive dining hall. The lady of the house breakfasted in her bed like most married women of the upper classes, and of Lord Trewithe there was no sign.

She ate sparingly then returned to her chamber, where she asked her maid to dress her in a riding habit of dark blue velvet. She waited on the steps at the entrance for a groom to fetch her horse. The tang of salt permeated the dank air, while a thick mist drifted inland from the sea, blanketing the lower meadows. The groom arrived seated on his own mount, trailing a pretty chestnut mare behind for her to ride. Primrose, an accomplished horsewoman, immediately ordered her horse to be handed over, whereupon she mounted deftly from the bottom step of the flight that led up to the house.

Ignoring her groom escort, she turned the horse and rode away from Pencullen, heading for the cliffs that ran along the coast between Pencullen House and Porthcullen Bay, determined to find her kidnappers and bring *him*—them—to justice. Her horse suddenly baulked, refusing to go a step further. Primrose, trusting her instincts, dismounted and walked gingerly forward through the swirling mists. She was lucky; she almost went over the cliff edge. Throwing herself backward from the precipice, she landed bottom down onto the coarse grass. Crawling forward gingerly, she shifted near enough to peer over the cliff edge. A ridge of wet black rock situated further down the cliff face, darkened with age, hid the bay from her view but the loud boom of surf, crashing powerfully against the ancient rock walls of this natural fortress, attested to the existence of an inlet far below.

Primrose manoeuvred back from the cliff and sat, thoughtful, while her horse grazed a step away, ears pricked toward her grounded rider as she chomped the damp grass. The horse heard sounds before her mistress. Primrose noticed the animal's stature become wary; she lifted her head, nostrils flared as she scented the air for newcomers. A muffled plodding, a muted jangle of reins and gruff male voices reached her ears. Primrose flattened herself to the ground. She glanced anxiously over to where her horse stood in the shadow of a thickly gnarled and stunted tree, its wizened branches twisted and bowed by the constant buffeting from sea gales. Hopefully, with this thickening mist, the horse might be missed by those who chose to travel so clandestinely along the cliff path in such inclement weather.

A mule train moved at a steady pace only yards from where she lay watching. Each animal carried four small barrels slung across their backs, two on either side. No prizes for guessing what they contained, Primrose supposed with satisfaction. She'd discovered smugglers, to be sure, but were they *her* smugglers?

Once they'd passed by, she hastened to her feet and moved to attach her horse's reins to the warped tree; she intended to return to retrieve the animal later. Pulling her cloak hood up and hitching her riding skirts, she stealthily trailed behind the last mule, keeping well back and out of sight.

Primrose was shocked, when they reached the edge of the formal grounds to Pencullen, to see the group veer off to the side of the house. What were such knaves doing skulking around Lord Trewithe's estate? She picked up her skirts, scampering from rose bush to rose bush, until she reached the outer stonework of the house. Peeking around the corner, she saw that a set of double trapdoors had been opened in the ground near to the wall of the east wing. Men had begun to uncouple barrels from the mules' backs. They carried them one at a time upon their shoulders, stepping into a gap between the doors that she surmised must have steps leading downward, deep into the cellars beneath the ancient stone edifice of Pencullen. She wondered how long this deception had been played upon her kindly host.

Her breath hitched as a tall imposing figure moved from behind a mule. Jago! Anger swept through her, and she felt like rushing the smuggler, wanting to batter him. Pulling back around the corner, she flattened her body against the wall. Sharp edges dug into her shoulders as she pressed herself against the stonework, her breath ragged. With fists clenched, she fought against the impulse to run at the bastard who'd so humiliated her. An internal struggle raged within, one so intense it brought tears of fury to her eyes which she angrily dashed away.

Not trusting herself to look upon the smugglers again without giving herself away to them, she turned and ran away in the opposite direction, sticking close to the wall of the house until she reached a path that she knew led down to the walled kitchen gardens. Through them she made her way out into the meadows back to the cliffs, where she reclaimed her horse. The thinking time this allowed her meant that by the time she arrived back at the stables, she'd decided to tell Lady Trewithe about her sighting. She was met by her anxious groom, who had feared that his charge had been cast over a cliff, a circumstance that would mean he would lose his position and most probably never find work as a groom elsewhere.

As she entered the house, Primrose inquired immediately as to the whereabouts of her hostess, only to be told by Darrent that the lady of the house had travelled to stay overnight at her nephew James's to arrange the upcoming soiree where the two of them were destined to meet.

Pragmatically, Primrose changed for luncheon then spent the afternoon in the library, where she discovered a fine selection of books on smuggling. A stoical believer in the old adage 'forewarned is forearmed,' she studied the books with interest.

As it was, Primrose did not see Lady Trewithe for another few days. She thought it prudent to ask Darrent for permission to explore the cellars in the absence of both host and hostess. She repaid her debt of coin to him, prudently adding another for his loan, optimistic it might soften his attitude toward her but if anything, the butler seemed surlier than ever. He did, however, reluctantly grant his consent for her to go below into the cellar, insisting that a footman accompany her. They descended into darkness, each armed with a lighted boxed Bougie candle. Once in the dank recess of the arched cellars, the footman lit wall sconces that shed an eerie, flickering light over the piles of goods stored in the cavernous space, deep under the house.

Rack upon rack of wine lay in the wine cellar. Bottled root vegetables lined shelves that led on to pickles and preserves. A meat room held suspended carcasses that dripped blood into stone baths designed to collect the juices used to make black puddings, gravy and sausages. Barrels of salted herrings vied for space with barrels of salted meats and then, excitingly, she stumbled upon a stack of smaller barrels, one of which she ordered to be opened by the footman.

Holding her candle high, expecting to see liquid glinting in the light, she was surprised when the lid was prised free to reveal white, refined sugar lying inside. She ordered another to be taken from the bottom of the stack and opened. This one proved to contain spices. Disappointed, she searched the length and breadth of the cellars but nowhere could Primrose spot the smaller barrels of brandy or rum that she'd seen delivered.

Irritated by her inability to detect the contraband, she stomped back up into the house, where she managed to corner Darrent in the passageway. She demanded to know what was stored beneath the outer trapdoors situated on the far side of the house.

"You are describing the coal cellar, Miss, and it can only be accessed from the outside. Now, if you would excuse me, I have tasks that require my attention." He bowed his head disdainfully before departing, leaving Primrose determined to look inside that cellar.

The inclement weather lasted all that week and so her plans to explore the coal cellar were postponed. Lord Trewithe had suggested she explore inside Pencullen House. She discovered the house was built in 1565 by the first Lord Trewithe, who was given the lands by Elizabeth I for his valiant services against the Spanish. The grey stone house resembled a castle from the front, with its two rounded ends with crenulated turrets, one on the east wing and one on the right. Inside the house, exquisite Italian paintings jostled with family portraits and centuries of collected memorabilia. Paintings hung along the walls the whole length of the long gallery and down the walls of the main staircase. Primrose found the likeness of the first Lord Trewithe to his many times removed grandson of today to be quite startling.

Her own family was descended from an ancient line but her uncle, the eldest brother of three, had inherited the title, while her father, the youngest of three brothers, was without titular nobility. Unfortunately the original Latimer family home had been burnt to the ground by Oliver Cromwell during the Civil War; ancient family portraits were therefore non-existent.

She headed outside after luncheon. The sea mists that had plagued them for days had finally cleared, leaving open a stunning vista across the headland. Pencullen was blessed by its position, set high upon this perch of land which offered up such an amazing panorama of the surrounding seascape. Taking advantage of the warm sunshine and fabulous aspect, Primrose perched on a stone bench to admire the view. Glinting blue sea stretched far as the eye could see to the horizon. She dawdled, taking much needed comfort from the beauty of her surroundings. Finally she rose and wandered across to the trapdoor she had come to look at on arrival. She saw they were heavily bolted and padlocked, the doors solidly closed to her. Cursing, Primrose returned dejectedly to the house.

Upon her return, Primrose was taken aback by Darrent's glib announcement that her parents had arrived. Apparently Lady Trewithe's invitation had been accepted. Primrose ground her teeth in annoyance; she had thought her parents would remain at Caulderstone, their heads held high, ignoring and defying the gossips.

Her mother greeted her, tearful and flustered, her father with obvious animosity. No amount of assurance that she was in no way to blame for her misfortune appeased her formerly doting papa. Icily polite in company, in private, he paced and raged at her, even threatening to take her across his knee, so incensed did he appear to be by the shame of her broken engagement. Primrose bore his fury with quiet dignity, mostly because she had never seen him quite so livid before, but also because she believed him fully capable of delivering upon his threat.

Her mother was surprisingly sympathetic, confessing to her that she, for one, had never liked Timothy Ponsomby. She gave her much needed solace, comforting her with loving gestures of affection. On the first occasion they'd had private conversation with their daughter, soon after their arrival, Primrose had been gratified that Georgina had defended her against her father's vitriolic, verbal onslaught. It seemed that now that she needed her mother, Georgina would raise to the occasion. She told Primrose that she had known this day would come, the day when Primrose would displease her father to such an extent that she would finally turn to her for support. She stated that she and Christopher were both so alike they were bound to clash but reassured Primrose that her father would eventually come around. She knew her husband better than he realised. He was flummoxed, and Georgina knew that if there was one thing Christopher Latimer hated more than anything else, it was being unsure about approaching a situation. He was a man who liked to be in command. When things spiralled out of his control, he floundered, and that was when his temper came crashing to the fore.

When Georgina had stood up to him, Christopher had instantly ordered her from the room, demanding she go and await his presence in their bed chamber.

Much to Primrose's consternation, it was obvious to her that her mother had been unable to sit the following day. She was utterly astonished to discover that her mother had been punished by her father but even more shocked by his change in attitude toward her, his previously doted upon daughter. This was the man who'd taken precious time out of his busy day to teach his girl to swim, had stolen sweetmeats from the kitchen when she fell from her pony as *he* taught her to ride, not allowing the hands of a groom to touch his little angel. Her devoted papa, the man who'd taught her to play chess as well as any man because he told her she was as good as any man. Christopher Latimer had always treated his daughter like a princess, the angel girl who could do no wrong. Where was that man, who was this railing tyrant who had replaced him? Primrose, bemused, could honestly say that she no longer recognised her own father.

Her relationship with her mother had always been difficult. Primrose felt ashamed of her past attitude toward her mother, copying her father's condescending tone of voice whenever she had spoken to her. She now realised that this must have marginalised Georgina, forcing her into the background of her own daughter's life.

Avoiding her father became Primrose's sole preoccupation. To this end, she decided to kill two birds with one stone and find her way down into the coal cellar. She snuck down below stairs into Darrent's butler's pantry when she knew him to be above stairs supervising the serving of tea and coffee in the drawing room. The keys to every part of the house and estate hung neatly upon a rack set on the wall. Each key was carefully labelled in Darrent's precise handwriting. She searched until she found the key marked 'coal cellar.' Pocketing it, Primrose hastened her way above stairs, leaving the house quickly before she was caught.

She skittered through the gardens, darting from shrub to tree, wary of the large windows that today felt like condemning eyes spying upon her clandestine scheme. Once she reached the side of the house where the trapdoors lay, she breathed a sigh of relief; she was now on the far side of the east wing. There were few windows here; none belonged to family or guests.

Bent forward, intent on unlocking the metal bars that held the doors shut, she was unaware of another's approach until a large hand engulfed her own to aid with lifting the weighty door. She straightened and stared at her father in surprise.

He raised a brow and gave a sheepish grin. "I'm sorry Rosie; I have been an absolute bear, haven't I? Can you forgive me my temper?"

Primrose's heart melted at his apology and his use of her childhood name. She walked up to him and he opened his arms to hug her.

"I should not have taken my temper out on you or your mother. I am enraged at Timothy, and that damned pirate who abused you and ruined you!"

Primrose sighed with relief. Having her father turn against her had hurt more than she had cared to admit. It was balm to her soul to be held in his arms, safe again in the knowledge that he supported and loved her still. "I am not ruined in the way that you suggest, Papa," she assured him for what seemed like the hundredth time.

He squeezed her tight. "I know, Rosie, but society will not believe that to be the case; people always think the worst. I hate Timothy Ponsomby for abandoning you in such a callous way! Your mother had to restrain me from calling the coward out!"

Primrose giggled, picturing her petite mama sitting upon her father's chest. "And just how did she do that?" she inquired saucily.

He chuckled ruefully. "By reminding me of the age difference, and by pointing out the defects of my failing eyesight—not flattering, I'll admit. I tell you, the knowledge that I couldn't fight for my beloved daughter did not help my temper one wit!"

"Oh Papa!" Primrose hugged his waist, her eyes moist.

"Come, dry your tears, I am here for you now. I only wanted you to have a decent husband, one who would love and support you, just look how well that idea turned out! Tell me, will you take this nephew of Lady Trewithe's to husband?"

Primrose nodded. "If he is a kindly fellow and I think we might deal well together, then yes. I am practical enough to be fully aware that this might be my only option if I want to marry and, Papa, I find that I really do."

Christopher Latimer gently cupped her chin with his palm. "I want you to know that you will always have a place at Caulderstone with us, Rosie. I can easily have a private apartment modelled for you within the house. Do not feel that you have no choice but to accept this gentleman's offer."

Primrose was touched. She reached up to kiss his cheek. "Thank you, Papa, that is very good to know."

Christopher stepped back and gestured to the trapdoors. "So, do you want to tell me what your obsession with the coal cellar is all about?"

Primrose leaned into him conspiratorially. "Let me explain…"

CHAPTER 4

She thanked goodness her father was there beside her when those doors slammed shut above them and darkness descended black as pitch. The overwhelming sense of smothering suffocation she felt would have turned her demented without his rational presence. She had been right in her estimation that there were steps leading down into the cellar. A stairway led them down into the dark underground space, where they were now trapped, all daylight from the opening gone.

"Primrose?" She felt him move beside her and squeeze her shoulder reassuringly. "Do not panic, for I told your mama where I was heading. I have no doubt she'll begin fretting soon enough and raise the alarm!"

She sighed with relief. "I am so glad you are here, Papa! Well, this definitely shows that someone here at Pencullen has something to hide. Did you find any barrels hidden back there under the coal?"

Her father had been digging with a shovel left inside atop the coal for that purpose. "No, not as yet, but now I cannot see a damned thing! Listen, my darling, this meddling of yours has to stop right now. It could prove dangerous. I want you to promise me that you will back away from this. I will speak with his Lordship but then we shall leave the problem for him to resolve. Promise me, Primrose, that you will leave it at that. These smugglers are dangerous, their very lives will be at stake should they be discovered, and I am sure they will stop at nothing to keep their secrets hidden."

Before she could reply, a voice from above 'halloo-ed' them. Christopher lifted the shovel and banged violently upon the wooden doors above their heads.

~

"I SHOULD PREFER to deal with this information in my own way, Latimer, and I therefore request that you do not say one word to anyone about our conversation."

Christopher Latimer acquiesced gracefully. "As you wish, my Lord, be assured my lips are sealed."

Lord Trewithe placed his hand on Christopher's forearm and applied pressure. "But what of your daughter sir, can she be trusted to keep her own counsel?"

Christopher stared pointedly at his Lordship's hand and waited until he had removed it before replying. "She will if I ask it of her. She is certainly a chip off the old block, as honest and trustworthy a young woman as you could meet."

Peter Trewithe moved over to the drinks set out atop the small liquor cabinet. He poured two measures of amber liquid from a decanter into a pair of crystal goblets. He offered a glass to his guest and Christopher accepted, holding it up to his nose. "Good bouquet. French brandy, I suspect?" he observed before taking a sip, one eyebrow raised in question.

"Ever heard the adage: *ask me no questions, I'll tell you no lies?*"

"Indeed."

His Lordship raised his glass. "Well then, a toast to the art of silence!"

Christopher took a thoughtful sip. He affirmed nothing. Silent indeed.

Primrose regained her equilibrium due to the fact her relationship with her parents was back on an even keel. They were there to support her, and the difference that made to her confidence was enormous.

Lady Trewithe discussed the coming introduction between her nephew and Primrose with Georgina, and between them it was decided that a formal family dinner was perhaps the best way for the two young people to meet.

On the night of the dinner, the house felt calm and expectant but not filled with a fizzing excitement the way most houses felt being prepared for a ball. Primrose appreciated the difference, and was glad that all she had to concentrate on that evening was getting to know her possible suitor.

She bathed languidly in a tin bath lined with linen, surrounded by lit candelabras. A maid had washed her hair the previous day, so it had plenty of time to dry. Georgina's lady's maid, Elsie, who always travelled with her mistress, came to dress her hair after her ablutions. She worked quietly, creating a soft becoming style that left some pale gold curls drifting down over Primrose's shoulders, designed to entice a gentleman's gaze to her displayed bosom. Her dress of dull silver gauze over white showed off her pale skin to perfection, candlelight caught the dull silver, giving her an almost ethereal quality. The maid threaded thin strands of silver ribbon throughout Primrose's hairstyle, which added to her enchanted look.

The admiration upon her father's face was all the evidence she needed to bolster her poise as they descended the sweeping staircase together. Georgina was escorted down by Lord Trewithe; his wife already awaited them in the drawing room, accompanied by her nephew, James.

Primrose entered the large withdrawing room, brightly lit by chandelier and candelabras placed strategically about the room. A tall, well-formed gentleman stood, dressed in a dark claret brocade evening coat, his shirt cuffs edged in pure white lace. His tight-fitting black breeches were tucked into gleaming black leather, tan topped boots. His dark hair was dressed in a lightly powdered queue, and he was most elegantly poised with his back to them as he conversed with Lady Trewithe. At the sound of their entrance he spun about, a white smile dancing across a familiar, wolfish face. Primrose stumbled, halting where she stood. The blood drained from her face as she pointed a trembling finger at him. "That man is the pirate who kidnapped me! Her words rasped. "Papa, please do something!" Christopher shoved his daughter behind him protectively, stepping before her. "Lord Trewithe, call out the guard!" he bellowed.

"Prithee stay calm, there is no need for alarm! I do assure you that you are safe amongst friends." Lord Trewithe's conciliatory reply incensed Primrose.

Anger hazed her narrowed gaze as she threw herself at Jago. The slap she dealt him reverberated about the room. He caught her wrist in his and drew her inexorably forward until she could feel his breath hot upon her face. "We meet again, mermaid. I am so pleased to see you alive and kicking, or should I say slapping? I spent several nights bemoaning your untimely demise, so it's good to know you survived your swim—a mermaid indeed."

She gritted her teeth at his mocking tone. "Numskull, the law will come for you and when it does, I shall laugh as you kick your last, hanging at the end of a gallows rope!" she goaded, inadvertently spraying his face with venomous spittle.

He gripped her wrist in order to force her closer, whereupon he lowered his head to her mouth, his lips searing hers. She struggled, fighting him. The fury that filled her was intoxicating, but suddenly her opponent was gone.

Christopher had spun him away from her, delivering a solid punch to his kidneys. Jago, coughing, doubled over. Georgina screamed, yanking her daughter clear of the ensuing mêlée with blows being thrown by both men. Four footmen arrived, restraining them. Overwhelmed by numbers, the gentlemen stood anchored and dishevelled, glaring daggers at one another.

"Verity, take the ladies away! I will summon you once order has been re-established!" Lord Trewithe instructed from across the room, his hand still clasping the bell-cord used to summon help.

Georgina and Verity argued furiously about the rights and wrongs of the match. Meanwhile, Primrose roamed about the music room, unable to settle. She was restless, disturbed. The situation seemed unreal. How on earth did Lord and Lady Trewithe's nephew become involved with smugglers? This was a family of the upper echelon of society. Her head ached with tension. She stopped by a bowl of roses set atop the harpsichord, absentmindedly shredding petals from the nearest yellow rose, oblivious to the delicious, musky scent of the flower.

The door opened and Christopher stalked in, casting Lady Trewithe a chill glance. "Please leave us. I wish to have private congress with my wife and daughter." He held the door wide, obviously expecting no rebuttal. She swept angrily across the room and out of the door without reply.

Primrose watched as her mother flew to her father. He held out an arm to receive her, kissing her cheek, but his gaze was fixed entirely upon his daughter.

"So, Papa, what did they have to say for themselves?"

Christopher disentangled himself from his wife, stretching a hand toward Primrose. "Come, let us sit for a moment while I explain what I know."

She did not like his calm demeanour. Where was his righteous indignation, why had his rage dissipated?

The two women sat either side of him but it was his daughter he addressed. "I have learned that all across this county, tin mines have been forced to close. There has been great hardship among the people of Cornwall, women and children have died of starvation in their droves. Men such as Poldrunne and Lord Trewithe overlooked the fact that local men were taking to smuggling in order to feed their families. As we ourselves know to our cost, taxes imposed on foreign imports means that things we previously took for granted have caused them to become too expensive even for our household—"

Georgina interrupted. "Well, I'll say! Not to have cinnamon or nutmeg caused Cook to be in a state of near apoplexy!"

Christopher patted his wife's hands. "Quite. Well here, however, rival factions of smugglers caused fighting to break out between smugglers and wreakers. Evil men, who hold life cheap, lured ships onto the rocks. The wreckers murder the crew and take the ship's cargo. They told me of one man in particular who refused to belong to either a smuggler or wrecker group—he gave up the names of a man he thought to be a wrecker to Excise men in order to claim the reward. However, he named the wrong man and a local smuggler Captain, was taken to the assizes and hung, leaving a wife and children destitute. Poldrunne decided that he needed to step into the breach to organise local smugglers, attempting to make them become more disciplined and efficient. Lord Trewithe decided to overlook this illegal activity, even allowing the smugglers to store contraband in his coal cellars." He paused and winked.

Primrose nodded her understanding.

"The thing is, daughter, it seems to me that you still have the same two choices before you. Either come home with us and I will have a section of rooms made into an apartment for you, or you marry Poldrunne."

A mulish expression settled unbecomingly over Primrose's delicate features. "I cannot believe that my *own father* will not report the very man who kidnapped me and has ruined my reputation!" she retorted.

Christopher grabbed her by her shoulders, leaning his face in to hers. "Had I been wearing my sword, I would have committed murder for you; I should have pierced his heart for his crime!" He shook her once and released her.

"I'm sorry," she apologised in a choked voice.

Christopher took a calming breath before continuing. "However, Poldrunne explained that he'd intended his men to kidnap his Aunt Verity, not you, in order to send a message to his Uncle Trewithe. I confess that I did not fully understand the undercurrents between the two men. I felt sure that something was being kept from me. Poldrunne seems to genuinely want to make amends toward you. He offers you marriage and position in society but this is solely your decision, Primrose," Christopher stated.

She paused to tamp down the tide of panic that threatened to overwhelm her. "In that case, I wish to speak with him alone," she decided.

Georgina gasped. "No, darling!"

"No! Absolutely out of the question!"

Both her parents reacted just as she'd expected them to. "I will neither return with you, nor marry him unless I speak with him alone. I shall insist instead on staying right here. I have no doubt that the Trewithes' guilt, coupled with a little blackmail, will suffice to gain my permanent residence here at Pencullen should I so wish," Primrose stated belligerently.

"You and Poldrunne appear to be one of a kind, you should suit one another admirably!" her father snapped.

"Christopher!" Georgina beseeched. She held her hand to her brow, as if about to swoon.

"Don't you start that nonsense with me, Georgie—you faint, and I'll paint your arse red!" Standing, he almost dragged his wife along in his wake. "Stay where you are, I shall send the smuggler here to you!" he barked over his shoulder.

Primrose stood open-mouthed, staring after her parents. Never in all her days had she heard her father speak thus to her mother. When she had been small and thrown a tantrum, it had resulted in her mother swooning, a situation which had frightened the young

Primrose into behaving. Not once had she for a moment suspected her mother of machination.

Moving over to the harpsichord, she began her nervous destruction of yet another rose. She didn't want to be seated—at a disadvantage—when Poldrunne arrived.

As soon as he stepped into the room she noticed he was limping. She wondered why she'd not spotted that earlier. She grinned wickedly at him. "Stubbed your toe, my dear?" she taunted.

He scowled. "I walked on a bed of hobnails; as well you know, witch."

She thought her peal of laughter almost drew a smile from him… *almost.*

She frowned. Why was he smiling in that smug fashion? She didn't trust him, not one jot! "If I should agree to become your wife then there shall be conditions."

He waited with a raised brow.

"Naturally, you will cease smuggling. You will never beat me again, and you will not become intoxicated with liquor—ever," she stated regally.

He walked over to stand opposite her, the harpsichord between them.

"I will not stop smuggling. I shall *spank* you whenever I feel the need and, by gad, I shall drink whenever I damn well please!" he admonished.

Next thing, he was covered in stale water and thorny yellow roses. One left a scratch upon his cheek and he rubbed away the water, seeing streaks of blood across the back of his hand. His slow grin turned evil. "You see how foolish t'would be to promise not to beat you when I am forced even now to school your wayward behaviour?" He took a menacing step toward her.

She moved away, keeping the musical instrument centered between them. "My father will kill you if you lay one finger on my person!" she told him fearlessly.

He spun away, stalked to the door before locking it, and pocketed the key. "You would do well to heed me, mermaid. Come to me now and I shall go easy on you. Fight me, and your delectable rear shall suffer painful consequences!"

Her answer was a shriek of pure rage as she dashed around the harpsichord with Jago in hot pursuit. He caught her with ease, her huge hooped petticoats and heeled silver shoes a hindrance to speed and agility.

He towed her to the couch but as he tilted her shrieking, flailing form over the back, her hoop sprung up and caught him a blow to the chin. Cursing, he withdrew a knife from his boot and, shoving the frame out of his way, he cut the ribbon that held it at her waist. When he yanked her upright again, the hoop dropped like a stone about her ankles. He kicked the offending cage out of the way and swiftly upended Primrose across the back of the settee, whereupon he shoved her dress skirt and petticoats high over her back. Gravity completed the rest, smothering her head and shoulders while muffling her squeals of indignation.

"Once we are wed, I forbid you the wearing of hoops, such ridiculous farafiddles!" Without preamble, Jago raised his hand and landed a heavy thwack to her naked right buttock, quickly repeating the action on her left. He kept up a furious barrage of swats, until his hand hurt and she'd stopped kicking.

He lifted her upright, grasped her by her upper arm, and marched her around to the front of the furniture. He sat and yanked her down onto his lap. She began to struggle and curse but he grasped her chin, crushing his mouth upon hers, kissing her roughly. Hands that beat against his shoulders slowly subsided as he deepened his questing kiss. Hammering upon the locked door turned to a cracking and splintering of wood as Christopher broke it open. He stumbled into the music room, followed by an anxious Lord Trewithe.

"Well, well!" The Lord chuckled upon seeing the young people clasped together in such a compromising knot. "A wedding it shall be!"

Primrose shoved herself as far back as she could whilst seated upon Jago's lap. "Not so!" she protested vehemently.

"As soon as the ceremony can be arranged," Christopher agreed firmly.

Primrose spluttered but she could form no word of protest since she found herself tilted backward and thoroughly kissed. Damn the fellow, he could melt her bones with such a kiss was her last coherent thought before her traitorous body took over. His constricting arms moulded her to him as her lips parted all too readily under his, her body humming with bittersweet desire.

"Fie, Primrose..." Georgina gasped as she stepped into the room and succumbed to her very first, quite genuine, swoon.

CHAPTER 5

No amount of reasoning, pleading or demanding moved her parents one iota from the view that Primrose hadn't been honest with them about her time spent with Jago aboard the *Mermaid's Tail.* They insisted she marry the devilish smuggler as soon as may be, secretly concerned she might be with child.

Primrose decided her best course of action was to leave Pencullen under cover of darkness and head home to Surrey. She would live out her days as a spinster in an apartment of rooms within her childhood home. Although the thought was depressing, the alternative was unacceptably terrifying. She would not let that beast compel her, nor have dominion over her. She would rather live alone for the rest of her days than gaze at his smug countenance for one solitary moment.

She laid her clandestine plan with care, waiting until the eve of her proposed wedding before disappearing. Lord Trewithe had obtained a special licence and he organized their ceremony to be held in Pencullen Chapel. A dinner had been arranged for the night before the wedding and Primrose knew the wine would be flowing. She planned to encourage the men to drink to excess in order they should sleep soundly that night. She begged her father to offer liquor to all the servants for their own celebration in the servants' hall. Lord Trewithe waved aside Christopher's offer and provided grog to be distributed amongst his staff.

She played her part well, since there was no Jago to distract or taunt her—it was considered bad luck for the bride to see the groom the night before her wedding. Primrose had quietly requested that the footmen keep the gentlemen's glasses filled throughout the meal, in order for them to have full glasses ready to make many toasts, and toast they did. No sooner had Christopher toasted his daughter, than Lord Trewithe toasted his wife's nephew, which in turn prompted Christopher to toast their hosts and Lord Trewithe to toast his guests, and so on and so on. As the eve grew ever later, the men began slurring their words and those words became ever bawdier. The ladies discreetly withdrew, insisting they needed their beds due to the morrow's early start.

By one of the clock, the house was silent and Primrose was dressed in her warmest pelisse and stout boots. The floors creaked alarmingly as she crept through the old house, heading for the back where the retiring and cloak rooms were situated. The dogs awoke from their slumber to greet her with thumping tails and wet tongues. She was prepared for their attention and handed out the meat treats she'd secreted in her napkin from the table at dinner.

She slipped out of the long passage that led from the boot room into the gardens. From there she made her way to the stables. Choosing the same gentle mare she'd ridden before, she tacked the horse. That done, she filled a saddle bag with horse mash and nuggets before leading her quietly out into the starlit night. They walked to the farthest part of the gardens, where Primrose mounted standing upon a low stone wall. From this far away the sound of a single horse's hooves could not be heard from up at the house should anyone be stirring.

Her plan was to ride as far as Truro that night, where acquaintances of her family lived. She decided her story would be to claim that she had become separated and lost while riding farther ahead of her parents' coach than she'd planned, and thus needed to seek shelter.

She'd not considered the problem that darkness posed, nor her own fearful reaction to the unlit paths through tree-lined rides and spooky pockets of deeply shadowed glades. Nor had she factored in the fear her horse might feel. A sudden blur of white flew across in front of them, screeching the eerie cry of a barn owl, whereupon the mare reared to her hind legs. Coming back onto all fours the horse took off at high speed. Primrose clung on for dear life. Keeping her head low as sapling branches whipped about her head and shoulders painfully, she fought to bring her horse back under control.

The mare careened around a bend then, faced with a fallen tree, she attempted to make the jump. Primrose knew better than to yank upon the reins, letting the horse have her head, praying as they soared that they would land safe and well upon the other side.

HER HEAD ACHED. Opening an eye, she squinted as bright sunlight blinded her. Groaning at the stiffness in her back, she rolled sideways, finding herself lying amongst mud and leaf debris. Of her mare there was no sign. Slowly sitting, she assessed each of her limbs for damage; thankfully she didn't appear to have broken anything. A hand to her aching head came away sticky, red with clotted blood. None still flowed; nevertheless, she sensibly took a moment of recovery, resting where she sat before attempting to stand.

All around, her bird song filled the soft morning air, the sun's warmth welcome after the chill of the late summer night. Primrose finally clambered to her feet. Stretching, she combed her fingers through her tangled tresses, pins scattering as she pulled her hair free, leaving it to spill wildly about her shoulders. Tentatively she began to walk, having no idea where she was, only knowing that behind her lay Pencullen and her rejected wedding day. Forward lay an unknown future.

The sudden pounding of hooves disturbed woodland birds into startled flight. Primrose was quick to hobble off the path. Scrambling into a bank of shrubs, she sank low behind her leafy bower. A black stallion and rider careered into the clearing. The rider pulled his horse up so short that the animal spun, using its powerful haunches for the sudden turn about. A man leapt from the animal's back and strode over to the fallen tree; crouching, he studied the ground. Standing again he moved slowly, turning, he gazed about him. Finally he straightened, focused on her direction. Primrose drew in a sharp breath as she recognised the man as Jago Poldrunne.

"Come out, mermaid, you have no escape through a porthole this time around."

She held her breath, he must be bluffing. Surely he couldn't actually *know* she was there... could he?

"You have earned enough punishment to keep you from sitting for at least a week. While I am more than happy to make that a month, it would go easier on you if you showed yourself voluntarily. Now come out from inside that bush."

Primrose hesitated, he was bluffing. Suddenly he strode toward her hideout. She squealed. Galvanized into action she turned to run but before she had even straightened, a hand grasped the hair at the nape of her neck, yanking her out from her hidey-hole.

"Why 'tis a pretty woodland nymph sent to pleasure me, the weary traveller!" he jested sarcastically. Pulling her into his chest and up onto her toes, he lowered his fierce dark gaze to her shrinking blue eyes. "I am weary, *extremely weary,* of chasing after you. I have been up since before sunrise. You sorely need a lesson in obedience but fear not, I shall be delighted to give you one, one you'll not soon forget. However, punishment shall have to wait until after we are wed!"

Primrose's eyes widened.

He nodded his head sagely. "Fear not, *heller,* we shall be wed." He clucked his tongue as he turned her head, studying her wound. Pulling forth a clean handkerchief from his pocket he wiped her forehead clear of dirt and dried blood. "A scratch, not serious," he muttered, more to himself than her. "Come, we are already late for our wedding."

He scooped her up and stalked toward his skittish horse, muttering guttural Cornish words at his black beast in his devilish native tongue. The animal quietened and stood docile, allowing him to unceremoniously shove Primrose up onto the high saddle before swinging up behind her. One arm tight about her waist held her firm against his chest, the other grasped the reins of his horse. "I told them I would find you; our families await us in the chapel. It looks as though you'll be wed in what you stand in my girl, for you'll not leave my sight again until my ring claims you as wife."

Primrose made to speak but his arm tightened fiercely about her as the beast leaped forward and the breath was knocked from her quaking body.

They reined up front of a small grey stone church that looked to have weathered many a storm over the years. The chapel had in fact been built long before Pencullen House. Primrose spat at him, then kicked as he dragged her from the horse. She dug in her heels, screaming insults as he dragged her. She fought so hard that he was forced to take a hand to her hindquarters whenever she came within reach.

The congregation turned as one, watching in silent shock as the doors to the church were kicked apart to reveal the tall dark smuggler. He tugged Primrose inside and threw her down the aisle before him. She was dishevelled and covered in leaf mould, mud spattered over her wild, loosely flowing hair. She looked like a mad woman as she attempted to scoot behind him, looking frantically for escape. He caught the pale skein of trailing hair and wound it about his brawny forearm, using that to guide and yank her along the aisle to the altar.

A nervous priest awaited them. The congregation held their breath; nobody had ever seen a bride arrive at a wedding in such a state before. As tension reached breaking point excited chattering broke out, reaching such a crescendo it drowned out the conversation being held up at the altar.

"I am sorry but I cannot marry an unwilling party…" the Priest stammered apologetically.

"*Gisson*, you can, and by God, you will!" Jago snarled.

Christopher strode across to his daughter's side. "Behave! Stand still, show some dignity, daughter, you are completely disgraced and beyond my help! Accept your fate, Primrose; be grateful that this man is willing to take you to wife!"

Her reply was a resounding slap to her father's cheek. Before Christopher could react to this shocking display of disrespect from his own daughter, a hand landed hard upon her arse—instant retribution from her furious intended.

"Get on with it!" Jago ordered the priest shortly, his patience worn thin. The trembling man hastily complied, chanting the Latin ceremony as fast as he could. When he prompted each of them for their troths, Primrose remained silent until a large hand descended upon her derriere, eliciting an enraged shriek which quickly morphed into a highly suspect response. "Very well then, I marry this pustulent dog under protest!" The priest completely ignored Primrose's contentious outburst and hurried on in Latin.

As he slid the heavy gold band onto her wedding finger, Jago clasped her bitten thumb and studied her mauled digit. He looked from it to her, an eyebrow quizzically raised. Flushing with shame, she snatched her hand away. They were instructed to kneel for the Father's blessing. Jago dragged her to her knees, after which the priest pronounced them man and wife.

Jago got to his feet and, still grasping Primrose by her hair, he yanked her up into his arms, smothering her noisy protests with his mouth. She was instantly made boneless, so that when he finally set her from him, she stumbled. He caught her and supported her about the waist as he marched her into the back of the chapel where they signed the register together with Lord Trewithe and Christopher Latimer, who stood as witness to their signatures. Jago guided the wilting, exhausted but compliant Primrose up the aisle to the church door. It appeared that she'd concluded that there was little point in further protest now that the deed was done and she was Mistress Poldrunne.

"Coo-ee, James, we shall see you both back at Pencullen House!" Verity Trewithe called.

Jago halted and executed a sweeping bow to the congregation, addressing the gathering. "I thank you all for coming today to witness my marriage. I am taking my wife home to Poldrunne. As you see, she is not feeling well. Please go, enjoy the wedding feast that I know my aunt has arranged for you. Good day to you all!"

Shocked gasps and murmured voices swelled indignantly as Jago shoved open the church doors and towed his new bedraggled wife outside to his waiting horse. He threw her up onto the back of his black steed, once again leaping into position behind her. Taking the reins he turned the animal and rode away, his arm anchored securely about Primrose's waist.

She was exhausted in mind and body and leaned back docilely against the plain of his chest. Her hand rested on his bulging forearm as it clasped her safely to him. She marvelled at the size and strength of his muscles, ruefully concluding that it was no wonder he was able to spank her so hard. A shiver of apprehension washed over her. She was married to this man and he was her husband now, which meant he had certain rights over her body. Nervously she wondered about lying with him in the marital bed—what might that entail? Already she knew he had the power to overwhelm her senses. He only had to kiss her and she lost coherent thought. To be held in his arms, possessed by him completely, now that would be a terrifying but also exciting experience.

Her mother had shared a little knowledge of the marriage bed with her but it had all sounded poetic and euphemistic rather than physical. Primrose knew that there was a giving and a taking involved between the man and the woman, but the how remained a mystery to her.

After thirty minutes of riding, they rounded a bend on the cliff and climbed up the rise. Looking down, Primrose saw a house sat squat in the valley of two cliffs, a grey stone manor house with a crenulated top. So that dour building was to be her home for the rest of her life? Her heart sank.

CHAPTER 6

As they drew near, chickens flew squawking from under the hooves of the great black stallion. Three goats leapt onto the low dry stone wall, bleating either irritation or greeting at the newcomers. Jago slid off the horse and lifted his bride down, setting her onto the ground carefully, ensuring that she was steady before he removed his hands from her waist. He nodded toward the porch. "Go inside and ask Kerra to make tea."

Could it be… "Kerra Tucket?" she asked hopefully.

He frowned as he began to walk away, leading the horse toward the stables. "Aye, why d' you ask?"

Primrose was already heading into the porch. "No reason!" she called over her shoulder as she entered the house.

Jago shook his head. She confounded him, this mercurial woman he'd wed. He recalled the winsome girl scattering petals across the harpsichord. He'd been moved by her beauty that night, looking so unbearably beautiful, clothed in her silver gown. Her thick fair hair gleaming about her deceptive angel's face, one which totally belied her acrimonious tongue. Perhaps she was a changeling, swapped at birth by fairies—or, more likely, mermaids? He grinned wryly… Why oh why had he been attracted to this particular wench? Alas, she was trouble with a capital 'T.' There were easier maids to be had in many a tavern from here to Land's End, so why had he wanted her? Blessed if he knew the answer but by Gad, he'd known he had to have her and now she was his.

"SAM!" he bellowed, walking into the stables. He found the heavy young man carefully currying the carriage horse's mane. "Conan's exhausted, possibly blown; give him a rub, plenty of hot mash and a blanket." Sam nodded, grunting an affirmative. Jago entered his home and halted as light infectious laughter lilted down the dark passage way. He liked the sound. Drawn toward the source of happiness, he encountered his curmudgeonly housekeeper hugging his new wife. Even more astounding, both were smiling, at least until he entered the room. He stood scowling at the pair, unsure how to proceed, baffled by this ostensible meeting of friends. Could this be to his advantage or his detriment?

Primrose bathed in the leaky, coopered wooden tub while Kerra scrubbed her back. She smeared ointment on the cut above her forehead. Primrose explained how she and Jago had met and for the first time she held nothing back from the telling, for she was drawn to and instinctively trusted the housekeeper. While she dried herself, Kerra prepared her a plate of scrambled eggs, served with hunks of fresh homemade bread slathered with golden butter. Jago had eaten separately from her, choosing to sup in the dusty dining room alone. He'd then bathed in her cooling bath water, while Kerra had taken her on a tour of the manor.

The house was old and dark, in dire need of a woman's touch. Many furnishings were so ancient they were falling apart; moths had made a banquet of most of the bed hangings, many hung in ribbons. The master's chamber seemed to be the least mouldy of the five bedrooms in the house; the crimson furnishings had at least survived the moth. The ancient Jacobean furniture was heavy and uncomfortable; there was not an upholstered chair to sit upon.

Seating in the parlour consisted of two simply carved, high backed settees, both with hard backs. The wooden seats had no cushions to soften the benches. Primrose decided at once where some of her generous dowry would be spent.

Darkness fell as sea gales buffeted the ancient manor. Primrose retired to the master's chamber, where she donned a linen shirt that she found inside a chest which she assumed belonged to Jago. Reclining nervously upon the heavily carved bed, she awaited her new husband. The moment she had dreaded since their marriage drew near. She considered running again but what was the point? Where would she seek shelter? No, this time she decided that she had to accept her fate and face her demon… And there he was, standing in the doorway wearing nothing but a loose fitting shirt, open at the neck, his damp hair dark from his bath, his eyes shadowed as he stared at her curled in his bed.

"Turn over onto your front," he growled.

Hesitating momentarily, she thought it best to do as he demanded. She heard him move across the room and turned to watch as he went to the chest. Lifting the lid, he removed something from inside. "What is that?" she asked tentatively.

His answer was to whack the side of the bed with whatever it was he held. The loud thwack the impact made had her jumping up onto all fours, ready to scramble away. "Stay where you are! I have tolerated much from you this day, woman. I aim to show you the consequences of such behaviour as my wife, and should you ever decide to act the harridan again, this shall be your reward. Lift your nightshirt, or should I say *my* shirt." His grim chuckle did nothing to ease the tension in Primrose, who froze in position, literally unable to move a muscle to obey.

"Primrose, such a misnamed wench, you should have been named something like firethorn. Although, come to think on it, your hair colour doth lend itself to your name," he mused as he stalked about the bed. Stopping by her side he smoothed his palm over the hillock of her flank, sliding the cotton shirt up over her buttocks until it bunched around her waist. He looked his fill, enjoying the sight of her pale flushed flesh and smooth curves. The only sound in the room was the soft splutter of the wavering candle and her shortened breath, which gave away her anxiousness.

"This will hurt... brace yourself," he warned.

Her eyes widened but she did not move a muscle as the air churned above her and a scalding line of fire fell across the crown of her bottom. Dear God, what was he punishing her with, a burning branch? She was not far from the mark; Jago held a birch, made up of three rope bound, sturdy twigs. His father had used just such an object to correct him as a wayward boy; now he used the same upon his errant wife. A high scream rent the air upon his second swipe and Primrose flung herself sideways, rolling toward the other side of the bed. He raced to catch her and when he did he pushed her flat into the bedding, his forearm across her lower back as he swung the birch high to lash her rounded rear-end. She screeched and bucked but it did no good. Grimly he imparted justice the smuggler's way... without mercy.

She twisted and kicked but he was relentless, and no amount of begging, pleading or sobbing halted her torment. Burying her head in the bed she wept, enduring the chastisement as best she could. It was a moment before she noticed the whipping had ceased. Her behind still throbbed almost as much as it had while she was being spanked. A hand grasped her upper arm and attempted to turn her onto her back. "No!" she shrieked, tugging her arm free, only to find herself lifted bodily into masculine arms to be held firm against his unyielding torso. A hand swept her wild hair back from her face. Her forehead was kissed as her body was gently rocked to and fro. A stream of gruffly spoken Cornish flowed over her, the gibberish soothing, comforting her as she released the emotion from days of stress. Tears soaked into his shirt front.

If Jago was shocked by the emotional outpouring the punishment brought forth, as he cradled the woman who had just become his responsibility for the rest of his lifetime, he did not show it. He shifted her in his arms, seeking her mouth. They connected body and soul every time they kissed; the world seemed to fall away as she melded against him. This time was no different. Once he was kissing her the tears halted. It appeared that he was content to hold her and plunder her mouth. His hands roamed over her curves, seeking out her most intimate places.

Primrose gasped as his hand closed over her breast. The powerfully delicious sensation of his mouth trailing his hand, his teeth grazing her burgeoning nipple, forced a groan from deep within her throat. Even her punished bottom seemed to morph into a searing zone of desire, one that centered heatedly at the apex of her legs. "*Melder,*" he whispered into her ear as his tongue swiped over her earlobe, nipping as he whispered in yet more unintelligible Cornish.

She found herself lifted, her shirt—no, *his* shirt—removed before he pushed her back onto the bed. Then the devil loomed over her. How could hands that punished so harshly bring the gift of so much pleasure? She watched his sinuous arm as it snaked down over her belly; his darkly weathered hand disappearing between her legs. She quivered. The delicious swirl of his fingers elicited succulent sounds of a woman aroused. "I love your abundant honey thatch. I like a woman with a good thick muff, one that I can get to grips with."

She cried out as he pulled her sex up with fingers wound deep in her maiden hair, tugging her sex to a tight slit that he released and pulled. She groaned with delight as he slid his middle finger inside her, teasing her virgin nubbin as he continued with his pull and release. The sensation caused a coiling that began deep in her womb; she panted and writhed toward some unknown precipice. Then he lay down and covered her body with his.

"I can wait no longer but I will try to make this feel good for you, after your initial pain."

"*Pain?*" she queried faintly.

Jago determined to see her settled here at Poldrunne, for that to happen he needed to make her happy; as such, he needed to make her wedding night as pleasant as possible. His liaisons with women up to now had been spasmodic, mainly due to his lifestyle. He did have some experience of women but never before had he taken a virgin.

Lifting the thick column of his throat, he braced his body onto his bulging forearms and eased his cock into her virgin channel. As he pressed home, they both felt her hymen give—she gave a squeal of discomfort, he felt an exultation that he had not expected to feel as the primal possessiveness of being male overwhelmed him. He took her, the joining sweet, but soon his need to plough her overcame the niceties of his intent to be gentle. He cupped her buttocks, plundering her ruthlessly, driven by the intense carnal pleasure. He was therefore surprised when he felt her nails dig into his shoulders, her teeth grazing the side of his neck, testimony to her aroused state. The rising crescendo of her unholy wail announced her pending bliss and her sweet, sighing gasps, coupled with the sudden ripple of her fluid sheath, brought him to fruition, spilling his seed inside his wife for the very first time. He shouted his triumph, the sound muffled by the dark, squally weather.

That night of passion cemented something deep between them. A bond formed: an acceptance of their attraction to one another and of their married state. When morning came, Primrose had lost the desire to run away from her life as Mistress Poldrunne. Indeed, she relished the thought of more nights spent in her new husband's arms.

CHAPTER 7

Colonel Guy French sat straight backed inside the carriage on his return from a clandestine meeting with his former general. He brooded upon his latest secret mission. Stretching out his long legs, he crossed his ankles and rested his booted feet upon the upholstered seat opposite him, grinning ruefully as he thought about what his wife Claudia would have to say about that. Claudia…

How could he leave her and the baby behind when he set off for Cornwall? He remembered how badly it had turned out when on his last mission he had been forced to abandon her. She had been kidnapped, stolen away, taken deep into hostile France. His blood still ran cold when he thought about how close he came to losing her. Guy determined that he would speak with her brother Charles and request that Claudia and their babe, David, remain with her family at Herstmonceaux House whilst he was gone. She could not possibly travel all the way to Cornwall with him. In any case, she would no doubt interfere, causing problems with his mission—which was to identify and apprehend the leader of the wreckers and the smuggling ring working too successfully in Cornwall.

Herstmonceaux House, Surrey.

"Apparently, Timothy jilted her because she was alone with a smuggler for a whole day and a night! I tell you, her reputation lies in tatters!" Imogene enjoyed the wide-eyed gasps from her audience.

"But how do you know it was Timothy who broke off the engagement and not her?" Claudia asked sceptically.

"Charles met Christopher Latimer at the horse sales last week and he told him everything! Apparently she had to be dragged to the altar by James Poldrunne, he is Lady Trewithe's nephew and—"

Imogene was interrupted by an indignant squeal from Claudia. "How *does* she do it? Dumped by Lord Trewithe's nephew only to marry Lady Trewithe's nephew! Honestly, that snide little harpy always lands on her feet!"

Margaret Wiggington nodded her agreement. "Her sort always does!" she said with a sniff of emphasis.

"Well it takes one to know one!" Rose Mortimer taunted.

"I was bullied," Margaret justified with another sniff.

"You *were* the bully!" Rose retorted sharply.

"Stop it, you two, we are talking about Primrose Latimer, *my* arch rival and enemy!" Claudia chided the antagonists. Rose and Margaret might have been enemies at one time but they were firm friends now.

"Oh come, isn't that a little harsh, Claudia dear?" Imogene entreated.

"No!" three female voices chorused in unison.

"Really, Immy, you are such a soft head!" Rose, her sister-in-law, stated with affection. "I just hate ill-wishing folk, that is all, and if poor Primrose..."

"Poor Primrose... *Poor Primrose*? Are we even talking about the same woman?" Claudia interjected vehemently. Primrose Latimer had tormented Claudia to such an extent about her lack of a beau that she had felt forced to invent one, a state of affairs which had set in motion a chain of events that led her to marry Colonel Guy French.

"Fie, Claudia, you should be grateful to Primrose, without her you might never have met and married Guy," Imogene continued, ever the voice of reason.

"Poppycock! I would have met him, actually I already had, but enough of this, come on, Immy, tell us more about that harpy's downfall!"

The ladies leaned in closer to their hostess, agog to hear more of the scandalous events that had overtaken Primrose Latimer.

"We-ll, there is not much more I can tell you. Of course Christopher and Georgina are extremely relieved that their daughter is finally married off after such a scandal. I understand Timothy is livid that she has still managed to marry into his family, albeit through his aunt's side."

"Has she a title?" Rose asked.

"No, it seems that she has married a lowly squire, she is plain Mistress Poldrunne," Imogene replied.

Claudia grinned cheerfully. "Serves the vixen right! she gloated.

"You have no title, Claudia," Imogene reminded her.

"No, but then I never wanted one. But prissy Primrose wanted prestige."

Rose looked confused. "How could she have achieved that? Timothy is a second son and a Right Honourable, to boot."

Imogene replied, "The Trewithes have no heir; they have named Timothy as heir to the title."

"But what of Timothy's older brother, surely he is entitled?" Margaret asked, intrigued by this unusual turn of events.

"Apparently he rejected the honour on the grounds that he already holds one title and is due to inherit another from a recently deceased cousin in Ireland. It seems he has no wish to take on the Cornish seat as well. After all, Cornwall is very far away."

Imogene had obviously soaked up all the local gossip. It was unfortunate for her that her husband Charles had chosen that moment to walk into the room and had overheard his wife. "I thought we had agreed that our neighbour's business should remain between us and not become the subject of drawing room tittle-tattle?" He concentrated a hard glare at his wife, who squirmed uncomfortably under his severe scrutiny.

Imogene was the most timid of this intimate group of female friends, one which had formed into the secretly named 'spanked wives society.' The group formed in domino style, as each lady confided to her friends her conflicting emotions about being chastised as and when she was first punished. Imogene was the least happy of the ladies about receiving physical chastisement from her husband. She was constantly vigilant, avoiding her strict husband's retribution at all costs. She was aware that on this occasion she had been caught red-handed and her heart sank.

Charles tore his irate gaze away from his wife. Remembering his duty as host, he bowed to the wives of his friends. "Ladies, your husbands await you in the orangery, where tea is about to be served." The ladies rose to their feet. "Imogene, remain behind, if you please. I wish to discuss your propensity for gossip."

It certainly did not please Imogene to remain behind but she knew that, should she argue, it would go worse for her once they were alone. The other women knew the word *discussion* to be a euphemism used by their husbands for a spanking. They cast a mixture of either pitying or envious glances at their friend as they filed out of the room.

Charles closed the door behind the last of his guests and turned to face his wayward wife. He noticed that she avoided eye contact. "Did I not ask you to be particularly discreet about the Latimers' woes? Did you not promise me that you would keep the knowledge of their personal problems to yourself?"

Imogene plucked at a fingernail, shifting in her seat. Already her buttocks prickled in a familiar way.

"Look at me when I am speaking to you, please."

She quickly lifted her head and stared at her husband. A shiver of unexplained desire caused her nipples to burgeon. Why did that deeper tone of voice and his commanding presence always have this odd effect on her libido?

"Imogene, please have the courtesy to answer me!"

She could feel a guilty flush flooding her face. She attempted to gain her composure but she was useless at any kind of deception. "I am sorry but I-I was only sharing news with-with, family…" she stammered.

"I asked you to tell no one, Immy. It is simply not good enough that I cannot trust my own wife with confidential information. I am disappointed in you."

Tears filled her eyes; she hated Charles to feel that she had let him down. "I am so sorry, my Lord," she whispered.

"You may be sure that I shall ensure that you are. Assume the position."

Once again Imogene didn't bother with arguing but stood and lifted her skirts and petticoats, then loosened the ribbon of her hoop at her waist, whereupon the contraption dropped to the floor. Imogene stepped out of the large frame, which Charles lifted to safety before he guided her over the solid padded arm of the low upholstered chair. He lifted her dress and frilled underclothes up over her back. Her bottom felt vulnerable bared to his gaze, and she shifted uneasily. The smack, when it came, was actually a relief. He was using no more than his hand. Her relief was short-lived, however, as the powerful slaps alternated rapidly from cheek to cheek and heat built like a furnace across her bouncing, fleshy orbs.

She heard her husband give a grunt of satisfaction. She knew he liked to spank her but he was a fair man and thankfully only chastised her when she truly deserved retribution. He had occasionally used a strap when she was particularly disobedient, which occurred usually when one or other of her friends involved her in their escapades. Imogene was a timid soul, genuinely wishing to please her husband, and she did, most of the time.

She was weeping and contrite when he finally stopped spanking her. His large hands roamed over her sore and tender flanks, dipping down to her wet divide because however she felt about being spanked, embarrassingly, she was always wet at the finish. She knew Charles was aroused and so it came as no surprise as the head of his pego pushed up against her slick opening. Imogene sighed with delight, this was what her friends so openly enjoyed, but she found it difficult to come to terms with her body's traitorous desire.

However, as he pounded her from behind, the heat from her chastened cheeks morphed to a searing flame between her legs and the delicious friction of his thrusting cock soon overwhelmed her. She cried out her pleasure as his deep baritone shout drowned her own sensual song. Leaning forward, he peppered kisses down her spine before drawing her skirts back down her body to cover her punished rear.

She hissed as he helped her upright. Turning her to face him, he cupped her face between his hands. "Have you learned your lesson, wench?"

She squirmed carnally against him as a reply. He chuckled.

"Have I told you how much I love you?" he asked, leaning in to graze her lips with his.

She smiled against his mouth. "You have a strange way of showing it, my Lord," she whispered hoarsely.

He chuckled. "You know I adore spanking your naughty arse whenever deserved. You are too well behaved for my taste, Immy. I prefer you to disobey me, at least once in a while!"

She pushed against his chest with her hand and he caught it between his own. "I haven't finished with you quite yet, madam. You will go now and take your tea in the nursery with nanny and the little ones. Afterward, you are to go to our chamber and await me there. I shall join you as soon as our guests have partaken of tea. I'll send them for a stroll about the gardens while I come and attend you."

Imogene dipped into a light curtsy and, blushing furiously, she fled the room to do her husband's bidding, knowing he referred to bedding her again.

Charles watched her go, a smile playing about his mouth. She delighted him, even after four years of marriage she still held him in her thrall. There was a light ratta-tat at the door. His brother in law Guy stuck his head into the room. "Might I have a quick word with you?"

Charles nodded and waved him into the room.

"So, you see my dilemma," Guy finished explaining.

Charles nodded. "I do indeed. Are you certain that you want to leave Claudia behind when you go to Cornwall? Wouldn't she be good cover for you? After all, we do know the Trewithes vaguely, and Mortimer is some sort of second cousin to Peter Trewithe. I suggest a house party, to be held at Pencullen. We could take our wives with us as cover and leave the children at home with their nannies. You will then have the back up from us should you require our help in the eventuality of any trouble. We all know how to fight. Wiggington is well known for his prowess with a sword. I trained in the Admiralty, as you know, and Benedict is a fine shot with a pistol. What do you say?"

Guy hemmed and hawed. Usually when undercover he liked to work alone, but he could see the sense of Charles's suggestion, especially since the Board of Trade and the Lloyds Register had requested his aid via his general as their intermediary. They would expect results.

"I suggest that you don't decide yet. Let us send our ladies to bed early tonight as punishment for their gossiping. I scolded Imogene for her loose tongue shortly before your arrival. I caught her red-handed telling the other ladies about the Latimer scandal. With them ensconced safe in their chambers, we can discuss my proposal without a fear of sharp ear-wigging for tidbits to share with others of their acquaintance."

Guy nodded his agreement. He certainly did not want Claudia getting involved with his search for wreckers and smugglers, not with her propensity for landing herself deep in hot water.

~

THE JOURNEY to Cornwall was an unpleasant experience for everyone concerned. The men rode during the day as much as possible to avoid their chattering wives. The valets gossiped with the lady's maids and by the time they were halfway to Cornwall, all the wives were fully cognisant of the Colonel's secret mission. The close proximity of the women over a number of days began to cause heated bickering to break out amongst them which, if left alone, would have happily been resolved quite naturally. However, two of the husbands, Lord Benedict Mortimer and Sir Thomas Wiggington, had undergone some very unpleasant experiences whilst travelling with their wives, Rose Mortimer and Margaret Wiggington, at a time when these two had still been arch enemies. They recommended to the other gentlemen that they intervene. The result was ladies with scalded posteriors bouncing along rutted roads in un-sprung carriages which, in turn, caused yet more fractious behaviour and more sore bottoms.

CHAPTER 8

Primrose took to roaming the sandy beaches and coves. Jago was gone most of the day and sometimes overnight. She became listless, bored in the house alone and so she wandered the shore, exploring caves or simply sitting on the sand, enjoying staring out into the distance of the mesmerizing sea. She didn't think she was unhappy, yet she wouldn't say she was happy either. She was in some kind of limbo but had no idea what to do to change her situation. Although she was inclined to want her own way, her parents had always guided and planned her day—albeit with things Primrose herself wanted to do. There had been a routine and a structure to her days that were missing from this sudden new lifestyle.

Kerra never questioned her or suggested that she should do some of the housework or take on any of the chores, although initially Primrose had spent time tidying and rearranging the house, making it to her liking. Stripping the moth infested hangings from every room including the master's chamber, she'd burned the lot and then sent away for swatches of soft furnishings to replace them. Kerra and she were working on sewing two long tapestry cushions to soften the seats of the hard settees in the parlour. Jago had insisted upon giving her a household budget to spend on the house. Incensed, she had demanded her own dowry, only to be told that the money belonged to him. He explained that she would have a monthly allowance for herself, and he gave her an initial sum which was to be spent only upon the home.

In retaliation, Primrose had spent a large proportion of the funds given to her on expensive gowns, which she ordered by post from a London fashion house. None of her new wardrobe had arrived as yet but she had experienced plenty of spankings since the beginning of her new marriage. She was now regretting her poor choices. She knew her bottom would resemble chopped liver when Jago found out what she had done with his money.

Sitting by the sea one afternoon, she ruminated for so long she did not notice the tide had reached her until her toes were soaked by a rolling wave. Leaping to her feet she saw the way back to the farther cove now lay under water. She was trapped in the small bay with high cliffs all about her. Studying the rocky shore, she noticed an area of darker rock set beneath a rock shelf. If she could make it onto the ledge she might be high enough to wait out the tide, which was at low ebb that day. Mayhap a boat would rescue her from the ledge? She hurried up the beach intending to clamber over the rocks toward the ledge but rounding an outcrop, she saw a hidden sandy path that led into a cave.

Primrose headed up the sand toward the cliff face, squeezing past the rocky outcrop that hid the cave entrance. Footsteps had churned up the dry sand and she wondered if perhaps this was one of Jago's storage hide outs for his contraband goods. She entered the cave but was disappointed to find that it seemed to only go so far back. Remembering the secret nature of her husband's illegal activities she decided to explore to the very back of the cavern. Sure enough, another deceptive line of stone hid the turn that would lead further inside the depth of the cliff. It was getting darker and harder to see what was in front of her. Nervously Primrose edged forward, she stumbled and stubbed her toe. "Godsdamn!" she cursed, clutching her poor toe. She plumped down onto the floor, frantically rubbing her damaged foot then realised that she'd kicked the bottom step of a flight of stairs hewn into the rock.

Once the pain subsided, she continued upward. The flight bent twice, as if she were inside a rounded tower which at the top opened out into a hollow room lit by a brazier hung upon the wall. Barrels stood neatly stacked against the walls, filling most of the space but leaving a wide path through them to the opposite side where she could see another shadowed stairway continuing upward.

Primrose chewed her bottom lip thoughtfully as she gazed about the evidence of her new unwanted husband's profession. So much had happened to her and in such a short space of time, she supposed that she must have been in shock to have accustomed herself to her present position of mediocrity. What had she been thinking? This was not the way her life was supposed to have gone! She should be living in the thick of high society with Timothy. Driving daily in Hyde Park, while dressed in the latest fashion, then dancing the evening away at Almacks. Attending parties, concerts and soirees, flirting in Vauxhall gardens then sleeping in the following morning, at least until mid-day; a life of luxury with maids and footmen to attend her every whim!

Tears of self-pity coursed down her cheeks. What a fool she'd been to listen to Lady Trewithe. She should have ignored her and her parents! She should have chased after her Timothy! She could have persuaded him to marry her, she absolutely knew that she could, she would have begged him even on bended knee. Now she was condemned to a life of miserable rustication. Buried in this godforsaken county, miles away from London, married to a goddamned smuggler of all things! She plumped down onto the floor and howled her fury, kicking her feet repeatedly against the nearest barrel as she wept noisily for her lost life.

As the storm of emotion abated, her tantrum wore itself out. She shifted herself backward and leaned against a barrel, feeling drained. Then the germ of an idea began to form. Surely Jago wouldn't want to remain living here once Timothy Ponsomby inherited Pencullen? She pushed away the sting she felt at the loss of the title and grand house she would have gained had she married Timothy. Instead, she concentrated her thoughts on planning an escape from Cornwall. She mused upon her new husband. She fully acknowledged that she liked bedding with him and was honest enough to know that she cringed at the thought of sharing that same intimacy with the spineless creature that was Timothy. Carnal thoughts of Jago unsettled her; her body thrummed, he intrigued and mesmerised. The things he did to her in the name of husband left her quivering with desire. Confusingly she enjoyed his delicious ministrations more after he'd taken her to task for some misdemeanour. Being spanked across his knee built within her an internal craving for his hand to rove her secret folds. Shaking her head, she tried to focus upon her plan. Her task, as far as she could see, was to seduce her husband into becoming so utterly besotted with her that he would agree to purchase a residence in—or near to —London.

Primrose assessed her behaviour to date. Being pugnacious and obstreperous, requiring chastisement on a regular basis, was perhaps not the best way to charm a fellow, or lead him by the nose. Or by his manhood, she thought with a base chuckle. Well then, she would have to alter her demeanour in order to convince him that he had charmed her and won her loving adoration. Once she'd achieved her goal she could wheedle him into moving them both down to London. If that didn't work, why then she would begin to cough, increasing her ailment slowly, blaming the sea air on her condition and use that as a method of convincing him she needed to be residing in the drier air of the city.

Hopping to her feet, feeling better for her scheming, she continued her climb up the stone steps. Upon reaching the top she found a wooden trapdoor and pushed upwards. It groaned but with a heave and a stiff shoulder, she managed to push it open. Surprisingly she found herself in the cellar of her own house. A reed mat set adrift by the opening of the door in the ground lay to the side. She straightened it, covering evidence of a secret door beneath. Jars of preserved fruits and vegetables stood on shelves that ran the length of the four walls, bunches of dried hops and herbs dangled from the ceiling beams. To the casual observer the sole purpose of the room looked to be storage of bottled and dry goods.

Primrose took a moment to brush herself down with her hands. She realised that she must look a fright, sand stuck to her clothes, cobwebs caught in her hair. Goodness knew how many smudges she must have across her face. She grimaced, she would never have dreamt of conducting herself in such a hoydenish manner whilst living in Surrey. She needed to improve her standards and behave in the manner to which she had been born. From this moment on she held her future happiness in her hands, and she was determined her plan would work. Jago—James, for *Jago* would never do in London society so from now onwards he was James to her—*James* would be back before long, and she wanted to present him with a perfect wife, one he could easily come to love and adore. She made her way determinedly up the wooden stairs into the main body of the house; she had water to collect if she wanted to bathe.

~

JAGO HAD EXPECTED HEAVIER goods when he'd been summoned by the drapers in town to collect packages recently arrived for them from London. The flat hessian sacks of what appeared to be clothing of some description had taken him by surprise. They were long and heavy to be sure, but fitted into the wooden cart easily when laid flat atop one another. Perhaps they were curtain material or even curtains, but surely there was too much material here for their simple household needs? He turned the cart for home and tried to give his bride the benefit of the doubt. He would wait to see what she had bought before judging.

He was astonished when he entered the parlour to find his wife beautifully attired and looking radiant. The room looked well, dark polished wood gleamed in the reflection of lit candelabras, the fire was ablaze, and he'd noticed as he'd passed by that a meal was laid ready in the dining room, which also looked to have been recently cleaned, the fire lit, its usual gloom diminished by the cheery glow of flickering flames.

"James, darling, you're home!" She sashayed over to him, her hooped dress shifting like a sail boat from side to side. He frowned. As she reached him she stood on tip toe and kissed his cheek. "Let me help you with your cloak, dearest," she offered, reaching for the clasp at his neck.

"No!" he softened his tone, "no, I shall hang it in the hallway." He strode from the room, pondering her sudden change of demeanour and why the conversion to *James* when *you devil* or *bastard* had done as his honorific up until now. Something was afoot but was this to his detriment? He returned to the parlour, whereupon she handed him a glass of port, again using the English version of his name, James. He scowled. "I prefer that you call me Jago. I thought I'd made it plain that you were not to wear hoops under your gowns."

She froze as she set the decanter back down and turned to him. He was astonished to see tears welling in her eyes. "You are quite right. I had forgotten, forgive me, *Jago*. I shall go and remove the offending garment immediately." She moved swiftly toward the door.

He felt a complete cad. "Primrose, wait!" Turning, she waited. "Er, hem," he cleared his throat, embarrassed, "I-I'm sorry. I shouldn't have spoken to you quite so harshly, not when you have made such an effort. Please forgive me and come back, won't you converse with me a little before we eat?" He held out his palm invitingly. She beamed at him and bounced back into the room, moving to take his proffered hand.

While they ate she entertained him with tales of her London season, describing the dances and balls she'd attended. He listened to her nonsense indulgently, thinking what a lucky escape he'd had being born and bred in Cornwall. How he would have hated to lead such a shallow life in the city. When she finally ran out of stories to share, he was able to mention the arrival of the packages he'd collected from the town, inquiring as to their content. He noticed a small twitch appear in her cheek and a certain tensing about her eyes. "I fear that I have overestimated the material required for making curtains," she finally confessed. "I have never ordered material for curtains before; can we return what is not required?"

He smiled indulgently. "Of course. Even if they only offer us a credit note in return we can put that toward other furnishings," he reassured her.

After the meal was over he offered to fetch her packages inside. "Oh, I am too tired to open them tonight, leave them until the morrow. I am going up, will you be coming to bed soon?" She sounded flirtatious, fluttering her eyelashes at him with obvious invitation.

He nearly laughed aloud but realised in time that he might wound her sensibilities and bit the chuckle back. "I have a few tasks requiring my attention first. Then I shall join you," he told her kindly. His shaft awoke, urging him to be quick. Once she was gone he dampened down the fire, snuffed out the candles, and went to secure the doors. Primrose had thoughtfully cleared the table rather than leaving it for Kerra to do in the morning. It would only take a moment or two to carry in the packages and place them on the table. It would save risking the material becoming damp whilst piled in the cart housed in the barn.

Jago stood, dismayed, surveying the pile of flounced and bejewelled gowns now scattered across the dining table, a slow burning fury flooded his veins. He'd stumbled whilst carrying the final load inside, tripping on the loose floorboard that he'd meant to fix but hadn't yet time to mend. The pile in his arms had tumbled across the floor in complete disarray, one wrapped gown had fallen open, revealing its duplicitous content. He had then undone every single package; each contained a rich and elegant gown from a well-known London fashion house. There was neither a single curtain nor any curtain material among them. Grimly, he snuffed out the final candle and mounted the stairs.

CHAPTER 9

Primrose preened, she was extremely pleased with herself; the evening had gone so much better than she'd hoped. Her husband had even seemed interested in her descriptions of London society and all that it had to offer. She pictured him in a London ballroom, how handsome he would look dressed in the latest fashion. His tall, sturdy frame encased in tight white britches, black boots and a satin coat of blue with high white cravat… no, she amended her vision, a coat of watered grey silk, yes, so much better.

So caught up in her fantasy was she that she failed to notice the object of her fancy standing at the end of the bed, his sardonic gaze fixed upon her face. "So you over ordered on curtain material, did you?" he asked rhetorically.

She froze, digesting his words as the blood drained from her face. His eyes glittered wickedly as he watched her squirm. Her tongue ran around her lips nervously as she racked her mind for an acceptable excuse. When one was not readily forthcoming, he ordered her up from the bed. She clung to the bed sheet, lifting it high as if it afforded her protection. "*Please…*"

"Please what… don't punish you?" he sneered. She nodded

eagerly. His answer was to tear the bedding off her shrinking form. She squealed as he reached for her, kicking frantically to keep him from catching her. He grunted as her foot caught him in the ribs, then he simply hooked an arm about her, lifting her from the bed and across his knee. He jammed his foot between the wooden bed frame and the mattress.

She lay drooped across his thighs, her feet beating the air with fruitless defiance. "Devil!" she screamed. He growled and landed a heavy slap on her naked arse. Several more followed then suddenly he tipped her upright. Grasping her wrist, he towed her out of their chamber, dragging her onward, down the stairs and into the dining parlour. Picking up a gown from the top of the pile deposited upon the table, he shoved it into her arms. "Put that on," he snarled before turning and leaving her alone in the darkened room.

Primrose stood, confused, anxiously awaiting her husband's return. She heard his approach, his heavy footsteps falling on the flagstones. Snapping out of her reverie she hurriedly stripped off her night rail. As she undressed she pondered upon the fact she hadn't bolted while she'd had the chance. Jago arrived clutching a smouldering spill, which he touched to the wicks of the candles standing either side of the mantelpiece. They caught at once, bringing flickering light into the gloomy room. As her head popped through the neck of the heavy dress, she noticed that he held a large wooden cooking ladle in one hand. Her eyes fixed upon the spoon, she took a step backward.

Lifting her gaze, she met his flinty stare. The look he gave unsettled her. She understood his intent even before he spoke. "Since you bought these expensive gowns, you shall wear each one as I punish you for your vindictive deception. In future, every time you wear one of these gowns, you shall recall the lesson of tonight. Now lift your skirt and bend over the table."

She hesitated. With an impatient huff he grasped her about the waist and, picking her up, he deposited her bodily across the table then yanked the skirt high up over her back. She winced as chill air hit the shrinking flesh of her vulnerable derriere. She wondered why she didn't fight him. Perhaps it was because she feared his wrath? Yet her conscience whispered the real reason. She was in the wrong, and bitterly regretted her mean spirited behaviour. Stoically she remained in place until a blazing smack landed against her backside. She howled and begged him to stop but as on the previous occasion aboard his ship, he ignored her pleas for mercy, blistering her cringing behind with punishing strokes with the heavy wooden spoon.

Suddenly he stopped. She sighed. The lesson had been short but painful, yet she had coped. She slid from the table with immense relief.

"Take off that frock and don another." With horror she realised this was how it was to continue until she had been punished while wearing each and every one of the ten new gowns. Weeping now, she shrugged out of her present gown and pulled a yellow silk ball dress over her head. He immediately guided her back over the table. "Another ten," he stated tersely.

She was astonished. Her previous spanking had been ten strokes; she understood now that it was ten for the number of dresses she'd bought. How was she supposed to bear one hundred strokes with that fearsome spoon? Panic overwhelmed her as she decided not to surrender but to fight for her freedom, convinced that she could not possibly withstand that number of blows!

Her kicking, screaming resistance was mediocre against his superior strength. It simply gained her another five spanks on top of the ten she received for the gown. Sobbing bitterly, she removed the yellow ball dress, moving on to the next, which had been her favourite choice from the modiste's fashion plate. It was every bit as spectacular as she'd envisaged, a shimmering gold confection, with a flounced skirt and low bodice which caused Jago to whistle through his teeth. "How much did this beauty cost me?" he asked with reluctant awe. "Spin for me." He twirled a finger. She complied; the delicate material floated outward with her movement, showing her bare ankles as she spun in a circle. "How much?" he asked again, his voice harsh.

She gulped. "Thirty pounds," she whispered, feeling utterly ashamed.

"Seven years' pay for a tin miner. Get back across that table."

Hastily, she complied. Her sense of wrongdoing grew, and she wept noisily as he chastised her reddening globes. Gown after gown she donned, until her backside felt like a swollen boil ready to burst, her skin burning hot as a furnace. Yet strangely, she no longer fought against his discipline. As she named the price of each exquisite gown, Jago made a comparison with some poor man's earnings, so that by the time her ordeal was at an end, Primrose felt ashamed, and knew she deserved every single blow he dealt her with the hateful wooden spoon.

Finally Jago lifted his wife from the table for the last time. He helped her out of the red velvet gown she was wearing. Tearfully, she reached for her night rail but grimly he shook his head. "On your knees, young lady, ask my forgiveness," he demanded sternly.

She obeyed, kneeling before him while gingerly soothing her tender behind, gently stroking her heated flesh with her hands. Still weeping copiously, she begged his forgiveness. His hand cupped her chin as he lifted her face so that he could meet her glistening, tear hazed eyes. "I accept your apology but I should like some sign of atonement from you." He gestured to his loins. Her gaze dropped to his fall, where she could see the stiff outline of his cock pressed against the material of his snug black breeches. "*Sug ow halgh,*" he growled.

"What do you want me to do? I-I don't understand." She was genuinely confused. He smiled his wolfish grin as he slowly began to unbutton the placket of his fall; she shivered with apprehension. Whatever did he have in mind?

His cock surged through the gap in the dark material; large, tumescent, only inches from her face. Gently he cupped the back of her head, gathering the skein of her thick blonde hair and winding it around his hand. "Open your mouth and take me inside. You will suckle my manhood and show me what a sorry little mermaid you are," he ordered huskily.

Astonished, Primrose opened her mouth but as he surged inside, panic welled. She gagged and he pulled away. "Slowly, gently, *heller,* this is not punishment but atonement. Take your time; show me with your mouth how apologetic you are for deceiving me." She tried again. This time it was not so bad, in fact, the bizarre act had the strangest, scintillating effect on her. She felt apologetically meek, totally feminine against his masculinity, almost worshipful toward her husband.

At first he was silent. Each time her eyes lifted to meet his, he stared implacably back. Then she noticed small sensual grunts escaping from him as she moved her mouth up and down his hard shaft, which pulsed inside her mouth as though it were a separate being. Tentatively she explored him, her tongue swirled over and under the ridges of his manhood, suckling his silken clad staff, enjoying the sensations of his flesh upon her tongue, intrigued by the shape and soft texture of the exterior of his iron hard erection.

His grunts turned to carnal moans and she sensed a change about to occur, his rod pulsed and leapt in her mouth. "I am going to spill," he gritted out between clenched teeth as his passion overwhelmed him. Her mouth suddenly flooded with essence. She had no choice but to swallow; in fact, she found the lewd act cathartic, giving her the feeling that she had somehow made amends toward him.

She stayed upon her knees; head bowed in supplication as he withdrew his handkerchief and wiped her mouth with a tenderness that surprised her. He then cleaned his shaft and tucked it away. "Come, let us abed, dawn fast approaches." He scooped up her naked form, carrying her up to their chamber where he gently deposited her on the bed. She moved under the covers and watched as he disrobed, admiring his strong male physique. The bed dipped as he joined her.

He gathered her into his arms, pressing his lips to hers as he kissed her gently. "All is forgiven, so sleep," he instructed, turning her so that her back was against him. She snuggled into his embrace but her sore bottom pressed against his groin. She hissed, shifting her hips forward, away from him. He was having none of that and hauled her back against his chest. Trapped, cupped by the curl of his large body, his arm slung across her waist, she sucked in her breath at the pain of contact. He laughed, tightening his grip, shifting her backward against the hard plain of his chest.

"Jago, I am truly repentant," she whimpered.

"I have no doubt. I know that you will think twice before behaving quite so badly in future," he answered gently. "Now sleep, I forgive you. It is behind us."

She wriggled in his hold. "It is certainly *behind* me!" She could feel the rumble in his chest as he chuckled.

"Sleep!" he ordered, but how was that possible when her traitorous body thrummed with need? She could not see that his lips had quirked in an indulgent smile, fully cognisant of her desire. She did not deserve pleasure and so he would withhold it... for a few hours, at any rate. He kissed her shoulder, holding her until she relaxed into his embrace.

Primrose lay awake long after Jago slept. She felt safe in her husband's arms. Her *husband.* She pondered the possessive word: *husband...* her man. Delicious shivers began to tingle down her spine. She shifted, enabling her to run her hand down his stomach, surprised as her hand closed over his shaft to find it thickly erect and twitching. Her thighs slid slickly apart as her fully aroused body yearned for him. She squealed in shock as he flipped her onto to her back then rose above her, taking her with complete possession. She sighed as she felt his length and girth stretch her so delightfully, his strong thrusts eliciting such overwhelming ecstasy that the cusp of orgasm bloomed at once as she screamed his honorific: *husband...*

CHAPTER 10

The following day, Primrose waited until Jago left the house, then went to find Kerra, who was in the scullery, sat on a stool, turning the handle of a crude wooden drum.

"What are you doing?" she asked curiously.

"Butter-r churning my *heller,* t'would do my old back a power of good should you take over the spinning for a bit." She stood and stretched, indicating that Primrose should take her place on the stool which she willingly did, intrigued by the process of churning.

"Kerra, do you remember that when we first met, you told me that if ever I wanted your help, I only had to ask?"

Kerra grunted an affirmative.

Primrose took a deep breath. "I want a potion or some such to make Jago love me; do you think you can help?" At first she didn't think the old woman would reply because Kerra moved to sit at the wooden table, pulled a bowl of pea pods toward her and began to shell them.

Primrose was about to give up and leave when Kerra spoke. "I'll need a wooden clothes peg, mind, and a small piece of his clothing and a strip of yorn, but most importantly a curl of his hair an' yours."

Primrose leapt to her feet, intent on fetching the peg and clothing immediately.

"Wait lass, 'tis not as simple as that. The hair must be from the groin, not from the head."

Primrose stilled. That could prove difficult but somehow she would manage. Jago had to become besotted with her so he would want her to be happy and agree to a move to London. There was a thumping from inside the churn, the butter had formed. Primrose watched Kerra, learning how to pat it into shape and place it in the butter dish; she impressed the top with a pattern from the embossed wooden butter pat.

IT WAS three nights before she was able to snip a few tight curls from her husband's groin. She needed him to be lying flat upon his back but mostly he slept on his side whilst spooning with her. Then she had the brilliant idea of piling blankets and quilts on top of their bed, complaining she was feeling chilled with the change in temperature of autumn air. This particular night he slept fitfully, finally throwing the covers from his overheated body, his naked limbs spread akimbo. Primrose stealthily reached for her sewing scissors hidden ready for her task underneath the bed, and she deftly took her talisman.

The following day she watched intently as Kerra turned the wooden peg into an effigy of a woman on one side and a man on the other. She stuck the curly hair on both head and groin of the open apex of the peg doll. She poured a drop of mead onto each of the faces, all the while muttering strange incantations in Cornish, before she finally held out the hexed doll for Primrose to take. "Place it under yer mattress and leave it be, soon he will love 'ee."

Tucking the strange charm underneath Jago's side of the mattress, Primrose prayed it would work.

A WEEK LATER, they were invited to Sunday lunch at Pencullen. Jago picked out one of her new gowns for her to wear. He had been right when he promised that every time she donned one of her new dresses she would remember her night of punishment. The dress he chose was blue, and the colour deepened her pale blue eyes to the colour of sapphires.

They ate shortly after they arrived, partaking of trout in cream sauce, followed by succulent, thinly carved roast beef served with a rich gravy, roasted potatoes and carrots. Dessert was apple snow and a pear torte, served with thick Cornish clotted cream.

"I have news that I think will delight you, my dear." Lady Trewithe laid her dessert spoon aside and turned to Primrose, who suspected her aunt-in-law held some secret up her sleeve; she had been positively glowing all through the meal. "Peter's second cousin Benedict Mortimer, with a party of family and friends, are coming to stay for a couple of weeks. I believe a friend of yours will be amongst their guests. Claudia French, she is sister to your parents' neighbours, Lord Charles and Lady Haffenden, is she not?"

Primrose's smile froze on her face. Claudia French, née Weston, her nemesis, was coming here to Cornwall?

"Primrose?" Jago prompted, looking anxious as she slumped against her chair back with silent shock as a million and one thoughts flashed through her mind. Uppermost was the knowledge that she hated Claudia French with a vengeance, and she most certainly had no desire for any re-acquaintance. Yet the presence of these fashionable, well-connected people could help further her plan to draw Jago back with her to London.

"Primrose, is everything quite all right?" her husband enquired again.

She nodded at him briefly before turning with brittle brightness to her hostess. "How absolutely thrilling to have such exulted guests! Do you plan to hold a ball in their honour?"

Lord Trewithe threw down his knife and fork with a clatter. "I bloody well hope not! Don't know why Mortimer should suddenly take it into his head to come here after all these years. I ain't seen him since he was fifteen or so!" he burst out in his booming voice.

"Now now, dear, do not concern yourself! I shall plan all the activities for our guests, and yes, Primrose, I thought perhaps a dance but not quite a ball might be just the ticket!"

"*What in Hades, a dance*? This visit is going to cost me a damn fortune, madam!" Peter Trewithe turned florid; he stood up and tossed down his napkin. "Jago, care to join me in a snifter?" he barked.

Jago nodded, a grin twitching his lips.

Verity Trewithe stood. "That is our cue to leave. Come, Primrose, we can discuss the details of the upcoming visit in private!" The ladies left the gentlemen to their contraband brandy.

They retired to Lady Trewithe's cosy private parlour, where her correspondence bureau was situated. She rummaged through the pile of paper that littered the top of her desk then brought a parchment of writing paper with her as she sat down next to Primrose. "Now then, to business. Since by the time they arrive it will be the beginning of September, I was thinking of a harvest festival themed dance. The ballroom could be decorated with two or three huge baked bread sheaths hung upon the walls, along with a string of plaited corn dollies. You know the sort of thing. What say you, my dear, or do you think the whole idea entirely too parochial?"

Primrose thought it an excellent idea and suggested basket displays of apples, blackberries and pears. "We shall have to invite a lower class of people than the Mortimers are perhaps used to mixing with but I always think the harvest draws people of all walks of life together and should put everyone at their ease," Verity Trewithe explained.

"I agree, and you may have no fears of the Mortimers mixing. Rose Mortimer is an American, she is a gracious lady, well versed in conversing with people from every class," Primrose reassured her. "Are those dreadful Wiggington hangers on travelling with the party? It seems that they are never far away from the Earl and his Countess, the absolute nobodies!"

Lady Trewithe looked taken aback by Primrose's vehement protest. "Yes, their names are included as guests on Mortimer's list. I understood that they were dear friends of theirs and that Thomas is a *Sir,* surely not a *nobody*? Or is that not so?"

Primrose ground her teeth; it seemed that she had to admit that almost everyone had a title except her. "No, you are right; he is a 'Sir.' His wife Margaret is such an abominable woman! Do you know that she deliberately tore my beautiful ball gown while Timothy and I were dancing at Claudia French's engagement party? For some reason the event was held miles away, at Merriton Hall. We had travelled all day to the Mortimers' Estate for the celebration, and this was how I was treated!"

Lady Trewithe frowned. "How very odd. Why should Lady Margaret do that, are you sure it was deliberate malice?"

Primrose nodded emphatically, omitting to explain the reason behind Margaret's behaviour, which had been a loyal act of vengeance toward Primrose for her rude and vicious treatment of Claudia.

"Well, well, we shall just have to accommodate Lady Wiggington's character as best we can. Please do not mention anything er, negative, to Peter, dear, he already resents the intrusion of guests. My husband is a creature of routine and habit, this invasion has him almost apoplectic."

Primrose nodded her understanding. "Of course I shall keep your plans to myself but I will impress upon him how much fun the dance will be!"

Lady Trewithe didn't look at all convinced. "Er, quite. Well, perhaps best not mention the dance, hmm? Thank you, my dear."

Shouting echoed down the hallway, reaching the two women at the same moment that a brief knock sounded at the door. Darrent entered the room, wringing his white gloved hands and looking flustered. "The gentlemen appear to be at fisticuffs milady!" he stammered.

Primrose and Verity Trewithe each lifted their long gowns so they could dash along the passage to the dining room where, sure enough, Peter and Jago were circling one another like a pair of pugilists, their fists raised. "Stay out of this, Verity!" his Lordship admonished.

"Stop this at once, both of you!" she cried. Ignoring her husband's command she ran to his side, grasping his fisted arm she hung onto it. Primrose followed suit and leapt over to where her husband stood grimly poised, fist raised. She tried to grab Jago's arm but he was too deft, easily evading her clutching hands.

"I don't know what this is all about but, James, I beg of you, leave now!" Verity pleaded.

"James?" Primrose coaxed. He glared down at her; she knew he hated her calling him James. She sighed. *"Jago,* please I want to leave, come home!" He gave her such an intimidating look that she lost her temper entirely and swung her fist into his groin.

Jago's eyes flew wide as he crumpled, gasping an expletive as he fell to the floor, wheezing a prolonged groan.

Lady Verity turned to her husband, who bellowed a warning cry of, *"Verity!"* Before he had time to yell a further threat, she'd landed a punch into the delicate male area of his anatomy. He, too, slid to his knees, eyes popping wide as he gave a long drawn out, high-pitched squeal.

Lady Trewithe turned to the butler. "Have the Poldrunne rig brought about. Ask Cook to make a poultice for his Lordship, and ask his valet to attend him at once if you please, Darrent."

"Certainly, Milady!" He made haste to do as his mistress bid, wincing in sympathy at the sight of the two floored, now dry heaving gentlemen but relieved that her ladyship had taken charge of the explosive situation.

"Primrose, dear, help your husband up and leave now, but have no fear, this fight will blow over. They have fought before and no doubt will do so again."

His Lordship curled upon his side, clutching his privates, knees drawn up. "Verity," he ground out between clenched teeth, "I shall take a crop to thee for this, see if I don't!"

She looked down at him impassively. "Very well, dear," she agreed, turning away to assist Primrose with getting Jago back on his feet. Peter Trewithe closed his eyes and moaned pitifully.

Once inside the carriage on their way home, Jago sat glowering at his wife. He conceded nothing, only grimacing with pain every time the coach lurched over rough ground. When they arrived, he clambered out first and held out a hand to assist Primrose. Once her feet were firmly on terra-firma, he tugged her hard up against his chest, his glittering glare burning deep into her eyes. "If you ever do such a thing to me again, I swear I shall take a buggy whip to you. Be thankful that I intend to take heed of my uncle's suggestion and use a crop this time. Get inside the house!" he snarled as he flung her away from him.

Primrose stumbled but managed to right herself. Once inside, she rushed up the stairs into their chamber, whereupon she lifted the bar and dropped it in place across the door, thus locking her husband out. Then, highly agitated, she paced the room to and fro.

The door handle rattled and stopped. All went quiet. Primrose breathed a sigh of relief which was short-lived when, a moment later, an enormous thump crashed against the door. Wood splintered as Jago burst into the chamber. He looked darkly foreboding and immensely unforgiving. Shrieking, she leapt up, scrambled across the bed and darted through the door.

She shot across the landing, almost throwing herself down the stairs, and headed for the kitchen, then down the back stairs into the cellar below. Yanking away the reed mat, she lowered herself into the darkness. Finding a foothold with difficulty on the steep steps, she grabbed hold of the trapdoor to pull it shut just as Jago's large fingers curled about the edge. His formidable strength no match for her, he forced the door from her grip. Primrose realised her only hope lay in outrunning her husband. She hoped that her nimble frame would prove faster than his larger body mass as she fled through the winding slippery rock channels that led her downward to the beach below.

Soon he was in heavy footed pursuit, his footfalls echoing all around her, causing her chest to constrict with panic. A sudden painful stitch in her side slowed her up as she came into the open area where the contraband was stored. A heavy hand fell upon her upper arm and she shrieked as Jago yanked her backward against his chest. His other arm snaked about her middle, holding her firmly back against his solid front. She felt his hot breath stir the hair at her nape as he whispered, "What to do with a disobedient and traitorous wife, eh? What are your suggestions, mermaid?"

Her answer was to stamp down hard onto his booted foot, using as much strength as she could muster. He grunted but instead of backing down, he swung her up under his arm and deposited her over a barrel, pinning her in place with a hand in the middle of her back.

"Tsk, tsk, darling, you are digging yourself ever deeper into a pit of pain," he chided as Primrose kicked her feet and waved arms that flailed uselessly. Her skirts landed over her head, constricting both movement and sight. She squealed, struggling as fiery pain lashed across her tender arse and froze her into silent shock, which only lasted until the next blow fell and then she howled. What the devil was he using on her? "No!" she screamed as more of the same scalded her rump. Kicking and wriggling achieved nothing, yet she kept up her struggle because it was impossible to keep still under such duress.

Jago watched his wife as she tried to avoid the fall of tar rope he'd picked up from atop a casket. It was proving a worthy punishment implement, possibly the very deterrent he'd been looking for to keep his harridan of a wife in check. It obviously stung like blue blazes if her violent reaction was anything to go by. Her bottom was already covered in dark red stripes, and he'd only just begun to punish her. The rope was going to be a godsend if it would facilitate keeping her under control.

His wedding tackle ached painfully where she'd punched him, but as his cockstand steadily grew, causing serious discomfort to his damaged stones, he cursed his lusty manhood. He was shocked that she had deliberately harmed him in such an underhanded way in such a sensitive and delicate area. Her un-wifely action severely wounded his sensibilities. The pain in his groin only served to strengthen his steely resolve as he lashed her repeatedly until his arm tired. She lay slumped, gulping tears, choking out incoherent apologies.

Seizing her, he uprighted her none too gently, setting her onto her feet. He towed her onward, down toward the beach. Once in the open, he marched her across the sand toward an anchored row boat. She kept babbling sobbing pleas all the way. *"Please, please, please,"* she continually begged.

Jago ignored her as he lifted her into the boat, dumping her onto the plank bow seat. She cried out and leapt up again. "Sit!" he thundered, pointing.

Weeping, she lowered herself gingerly back down onto the wood, crying out piteously as her punished bottom hit the plank. He grasped the side of the boat and pushed it forward into the surf, his biceps bulging as he guided the vessel onward until he was waist deep in water and they were well beyond the shore line. He clambered aboard; taking up the oars, he rowed them out to sea. Primrose continued to mutter pleas through chattering teeth. He glanced over at her, realising at once that she was terrified. Her frantic pleadings finally sank in; he was shocked to hear her beg him not to cast her into the sea.

He grinned. "Are you not a mermaid then, sent by Davy Jones to plague me?"

She shook her head in frantic denial. "No, Jago, I am only me, your wife. Although I can swim, I-I cannot explain how I was saved last time. I beg of you, have pity on me! I promise never to hit you again, I do really… I promise—"

"Primrose…" He attempted to interrupt but she began her pleading again. "Primrose, stop!" he finally boomed. She froze, staring at him with wide fearful eyes. He felt a cad for scaring her so. "Calm down, Primrose, I am simply taking us out to the *Mermaid's Tail.* I have no intention of casting you into the sea."

She visibly relaxed. "Oh," she answered in a small voice. She appeared to settle, perhaps accepting her fate now she knew he had no plans to throw her to the fishes. He shook his head wryly as she huddled in the bow of the boat, continually chewing her mangled thumbnail, until they reached the ship's side.

CHAPTER 11

Jago carried his wife below to his cabin, ignoring the fulsome cries of welcome from his crew. There, he laid her gently upon the bed before he turned and left the room.

She curled on her side, drawing her legs up to her chest. He returned but she stubbornly kept her face turned away from him, starting when she felt his firm but gentle touch as he turned her onto her stomach. She moaned and hissed as he moved her. Shushing her, he lifted her gown up over her back to expose her red, swollen bottom to his gaze.

She was covered in livid, flaming stripes. He reached for a rag and dipped it in the bowl of seawater he'd fetched, then wrung the cloth out over her enflamed globes. She hissed as the cold salt water dripped onto her skin, soothing her chastened flesh. He kept up his actions for a good few minutes, finally opening out the wet square cloth and laying it across her buttocks. She winced but quietly accepted his ministrations.

"We cannot go on like this, Primrose. You genuinely believed that I would cast you into the sea; there is no trust between us. I need a wife I can trust, and one who trusts me."

She turned her head to look at him. "You can trust me," she proclaimed, indignant.

"For all I know, you have damaged me for life, and yet you tell me I can trust you? I think not."

Glaring at him, she jerked up onto her elbows. "Jago, you were fighting your uncle. Tell me, what exactly was I supposed to do?"

He leapt abruptly to his feet and began to pull his shirt over his head. She stared at him suspiciously. "Whatever are you doing?" she asked nervously.

"I am going for a swim in the sea to cool my aching stones. You'll be damn lucky to conceive a child with me after the punch you dealt below the belt, you wretched witch!" He lowered his britches, revealing his enormously swollen testicles, she giggled at the incongruous sight. He glowered furiously and slammed out of the cabin, completely nude apart from his knee-high boots.

He stayed in the undulating sea as long as he could to allow the cold salt water to reduce the puffiness of his swelling groin. While he swam lazily around his ship, he pondered the dilemma of his wife. Somehow they needed to find common ground. He thought loyalty might be a good starting point. He wondered what Primrose actually wanted from their marriage. Perhaps it was time he asked her that very question.

He found his wife lying on her belly, her head to the side, cheek cupped in her palm. She was awake but remained quiet as he dried himself off and donned a clean but loose shirt that covered his privates. He made no attempt to pull on his britches. He perched on the bed beside her.

"Primrose, how do you see our marriage progressing?" he asked.

She hummed thoughtfully for a moment. "I would like us to move to London or nearby."

Whatever he was expecting her to say, it wasn't that. He felt disappointed. "Why London?"

She rolled her eyes. "Because I want to be a part of fashionable society, of course!"

He frowned. "I see. Very well, how about next year, we travel down and spend a few weeks in London for the season?"

She sat up with excitement, squealing as her scalded rump pressed into the bed. She hopped off the bed too quickly and tilted, staggering. Jago caught her before she pitched over. "Thank you," she gasped.

He wasn't sure if her thanks were for catching her or suggesting they go to London, he decided to take her thanks for both.

"What about children?" He watched her face as he asked the question.

"I expect we shall have some." She shrugged.

"Is that your total expectation from our marriage?" he pressed. She shifted uneasily. "Primrose?" Her thumb found its way back into her mouth. "Stop that!" He pulled her hand away from her jaw.

"I, um, you, um…" she faltered.

"Yes?" he encouraged.

She lowered her gaze. "You don't love me," she complained.

"Nor have you made it easy for me to love you," he countered.

Neither spoke, an uneasy silence stretched out. How could he explain the jumble of emotions she evoked within his chest, but could he say he loved her? He wanted her, oh yes, he only had to look at her, breathe in her womanly scent, catch her eyeing him with those wide blue eyes or witness the tilt of those bee-stung lips, to desire her. He drew her close; she leaned against the length of his body. Tilting her chin, he pressed his lips against her mouth, grazing her sensitive lips, sweetly, with tenderness. She responded, her breath a soft sigh against his lips, yielding to him so that his arms slipped about her tightening, cradling her lithe form.

When he broke the kiss, he lifted his head to study her face. "I want us to start again, to become considerate of one another's needs. I want your loyalty, trust and obedience, Primrose. What do you want in return, apart from a mere jaunt to London?" His thumb swept back and forth over her plump bottom lip as he spoke.

She found it difficult to concentrate, let alone reply. Placing her hand over his wrist, she stilled his distracting hand. "I don't want to be spanked—" she began, interrupted by his bark of laughter.

"Uh-uh that is non-negotiable!" He wagged a finger under her nose.

Scowling, she huffed, "Why ask me then?"

He chuckled. "Are you hungry?" he said, abruptly changing the subject.

"No!" she declared, crossing her arms over her chest in a snit. The sudden rumbling of her stomach belied her statement.

He kissed her firmly on the lips and set her aside. "I'll fetch us some victuals," he told her, striding from the cabin, still naked below his shirt apart from his boots.

After he'd closed the door behind him, Primrose wandered over to the porthole. She gazed out to sea, pondering his conciliatory words. What *did* she want from their marriage?

Up until now, all she'd thought about was getting back to London, but what else did she desire? He'd asked about children, yes, she supposed that she did want a child but in due course. What she didn't want was to become Timothy's poor neighbour. She shuddered at the thought of having to curtsy to him and his wife whenever they drove past her, no doubt ensconced in a much larger and newer carriage than her husband could ever afford. She wondered if Jago would understand her discontent about living so close to the man who'd cast her aside with such easy insouciance. Of course she realised it might be many years before Lord Peter Trewithe died, but knowing that when he had gone Timothy would inherit, was nevertheless a black cloud that hung over her.

She wondered how she would feel if circumstances prevented Timothy from inheriting Pencullen. She realised that under those conditions she might be happy living here in Cornwall with Jago. They could still take a regular jaunt into London during the season but Jago's smuggling bothered her. He spoke of trust, but what if they had children and their father was hanged for his illegal activities? What would become of them all? Primrose determined to discuss the way her husband made his living. She would suggest he turn his hand to something more befitting a Squire.

"THANK GOD, we should arrive at Pencullen tomorrow! If I have to spend one more night in a beastly tavern, I shall simply expire!" Rose declared.

"Mind you, one benefit of being less than private is your husband has no opportunity to chastise you," Claudia piped up gleefully.

Imogene nodded her agreement, while Rose and Margaret looked comically surprised. They both chorused, *"Beg pardon?"*

Imogene and Claudia gazed interestedly at their friends. "You have been spanked since that night we arrived at, oh, what was it called... the third inn?" Claudia asked in her usual forthright manner.

"The King's head," Imogene remembered.

"You *haven't*? Not even after calling Guy a *'pustulent boil on your bum,'* yesterday after we arrived at the inn when he was scolding you for snapping at Lester?" Margaret asked.

Claudia's eyes flew wide with embarrassment.

"Oh yes, I heard you quite clearly through the paper thin walls of the Roosters Tavern last night," Margaret informed her smugly.

"Guy was shocked at how much we could hear through the thin walls of the King's Head on the night we were all taken to task for bickering over whose turn it was to sit beside the carriage window. Since then he has been keeping a tally but I hope he will forget about *that* particular remark," Claudia acknowledged.

"I shouldn't count on it!" Margaret snorted. "Thomas never forgets any of my snide insults."

Rose lifted the hem of her gown and stuck out her leg. "Benedict has become very accomplished at devising torturous ways to make me suffer when I scold ever since he discovered that I was once again *enceinte*." She drew her skirts higher as the ladies leaned down to stare at her calf, which was covered in the faintest of tiny pink stripes.

"Ooo, do they sting?" Imogene asked. She was the least robust of them all when it came to punishment,

"Actually, no, they itch like a thousand little insect bites. I just want to constantly scratch." Rose immediately began to demonstrate and scratch the area; she then extended her other leg and began to frantically scratch that one too.

"What did he use?" Margaret asked interestedly.

"A toy switch?" Claudia giggled.

"No, but close; a horse tail-hair fly whisk a friend brought Benedict back from India last Christmastide." She lowered her voice to a whisper, recalling that their gentlemen were only a step away, behind a curtain, drinking in the tap room. "He has threatened to use it on my breasts if I don't curb my complaining tongue!"

Imogene gasped with horror. Rose's husband was her brother; she simply hated hearing these intimate things about her sibling and his wife. Margaret and Claudia looked at one another with wickedly shining eyes, they were both rather fond of ingenious punishments their respective husbands came up with and this titillating threat was a new one to them both.

"So, Margaret, are you intimating that Sir Thomas has spanked you while we over-nighted at one of the coaching inns?" Rose asked, dropping her skirts back down to decorous ground level.

Margaret nodded. "Almost every one of them," she declared ruefully.

"But why haven't we heard any noise?" Imogene asked.

"Well," Margaret began. The ladies leaned in close, intrigued. "He took me outside to our coach after all of you had retired for the night and chastised me inside our carriage."

The ladies cast glances at one another. Each lady felt instantly grateful to be married to her own dear spouse. Sir Thomas was certainly the strictest husband amongst their group of friends but by the same count, they knew that Margaret needed his stern approbation to keep her from becoming the unmitigated shrew she was before she'd married the man. Much giggling and whispering ensued, which attracted the attention of their husbands who came en masse to guide their ladies to bed.

Thus it was that every upstairs window of the tavern was filled with the curious faces of the Wiggingtons' friends as they watched with eager anticipation to see whether he would take his lady out after dark for punishment. The wives could not resist sharing this juicy titbit of information with their husbands. They, too, wanted to see if their friend would take advantage of the cover of darkness to clandestinely chastise his harridan wife. Sure enough, he emerged soon after they had all retired. They watched as Sir Thomas handed her into the privacy of the unhitched carriage. None of the women shared the fact that the knowledge of their friend being spanked had titillated their spouse's libido, ensuring every one of them enjoyed a lusty ride that night, which included the Lady Margaret.

CHAPTER 12

It was a huge relief to everyone, most especially the personal maids and valets who were squashed into coaches with the plethora of luggage, when the creaking, groaning convoy finally pulled up at the steps of Pencullen House. They had arrived mid-afternoon, after a gruelling journey from the far south east of England to the far western reaches of the English shore.

Lady Trewithe greeted her guests with a gracious welcome, then she sent an urgent message, via a footman, requesting her husband's presence immediately. She knew Peter would be skulking, hiding somewhere in an attempt to ignore their guests' arrival. Group introductions were made before she guided them into the withdrawing room, where Darrent supervised the serving of tea.

Meanwhile the coaches lumbered onward around to the back of the house, onto the large gravelled turning area where the Pencullen servants received visiting staff. They were only shown to their temporary quarters once their masters' and mistresses' luggage was safely stowed. Each trunk was labelled and listed, along with all the jewellery, which was stored in the house strong box. Pistols and other weapons also needed to be noted before they could be securely locked away in the armoury. An ink drawn map of the house layout was pinned to a wall in the staff corridor. Every visiting servant was urged to study the map. After the staff completed their tasks, they were invited for a cup of tea, bread, butter and gooseberry jam, which were served in the servant's hall.

By now the elaborate upstairs tea had finished. Darrent appeared below stairs to formally welcome the visiting servants and instruct them on Pencullen house rules. The valets and personal maids had barely time to down their tea before bells rang forcing them to abandon their break to attend to their employers' needs upstairs. Cook, who had been busily making as many meals in advance as she could, was working flat out in order to feed the greatly increased household. Despite the extra work load there was a buzz of excitement below stairs, and a sense of excited anticipation among the staff about the up and coming dance that everyone except Peter Trewithe knew to be a ball.

Upstairs, Claudia's personal maid, Lester, stood outside her mistress's chamber as though guarding the door. In a sense she was doing exactly that because standing where she was, she could quite clearly hear the sounds of distress echoing from within. It seemed that Claudia's confident assurance that her husband would miscount the tally for her misconduct during their long journey was proven erroneous.

At dinner that night, there were a number of squirming bottoms seated upon Chippendale chairs, and none of these posteriors were male.

"I understand you are acquainted with my new niece-in-law, Lady Haffenden?" Verity Trewithe opened the conversation. There was an inelegant snort from across the table. "Mistress French?" Verity turned her polite smile to Claudia, who tried but failed to look innocent. Guy cast his wife a warning frown. The last thing he needed for the success of this mission was his wife antagonising their hosts on their very first night.

"Oh yes, of course, we *all* know *dearest, sweetest* Primrose," Claudia gushed insincerely.

Lord Trewithe harrumphed. "I can tell that you, too, have had confrontation with that little hellcat." He winked sagely.

Imogene quickly attempted to smooth over any ill feelings Claudia may have aroused. "I would never describe poor Primrose as a *hellcat*. The young lady we know is propriety itself, Lord Trewithe. We..." she gestured about the table, "maintain that the rumours circling the ton are no more than malicious gossip, do we not?" Again she cast her gaze over friends and family.

All but her husband Charles refused to meet her eye. The other ladies shuffled uncomfortably, feeling coerced. Nevertheless, through loyalty to their sister-in-law and friend, they mumbled their half-hearted agreement.

Lord Trewithe harrumphed again as he tucked into his goose with hearty enjoyment. He knew what he knew, and no one would alter his view of Mistress Primrose Poldrunne! The only good thing about staying guests was the improvement in victuals served at table. The cost of guests however had him feeling decidedly liverish. He scowled as his eye settled upon the table centre piece, an elegantly designed tier of exotic fruit, topped by a rare pineapple. The thing cost him more than his thoroughbred horse to nurture and grow in the overheated pinery-vinery at Pencullen. Still, at least they could rent the thing out to other houses who wished to impress, once they were rid of this wretched company! He glowered about the table at his guests before returning to his plate; delicious quality dishes did go some way to assuaging his inconvenience.

"We are keen to hear Primrose's own account of her adventures, Lady Trewithe," Rose adroitly picked up the thread of conversation.

"Well then, you will be delighted to hear that I have arranged a picnic for the morrow, when my nephew and niece-in-law shall be joining us."

"Wonderful!" Claudia enthused falsely, then jumped as her

husband's hand gripped her knee under the table with evident rebuke. She glanced sideways at him and read the threat in his furrowed brow.

Thereafter, the talk moved on to much safer topics of conversation. Verity Trewithe explained the schedule of entertainment she had organised for the duration of their visit, outlining her plans for a harvest festival-themed dance.

~

ABOARD THE *MERMAID*, Jago suggested they got some sleep. They lay upon the cabin bed, Jago on his back, legs apart to ease his aching, swollen groin. Primrose was on her front atop the covers; her blazing buttocks throbbed to such an extent that she couldn't bear anything touching her scorched flesh. The sound of creaking wood as the *Mermaid's Tail* settled for the night, together with the occasional muffled call from the night watch, and the gentle slap of water against the ship's sides, lulled them both to drowsiness.

"What would turn you away from smuggling?" Primrose eventually asked, sensing he was awake. At first she thought he wouldn't reply.

"I have asked myself that question but it is not just about my welfare, it is about the whole community. I watched as strong men wept, burying their children. Whole families died from starvation and disease after men were turned off as the tin mines closed. It is a sight I never wish to see again, and unless I can find legitimate employment for my men, I shall be compelled to carry on smuggling."

Primrose sighed. "You spoke of children dying and I agree with you that should never happen, but what of our own future children? What would become of me—and them—should you end up swinging from a gibbet?"

Jago shifted, and began to play with a tendril of her hair. "'Tis hard for me to make you any promises, Primrose. Be assured that I am very careful, but should things become difficult with the Excise men, then I promise I shall lie low until they are gone. One day, prosperity may return to this area, and in that instance I could go back to being simply the Squire of Poldrunne. Until such time, I cannot legislate for what life will bring, do you understand?" he asked gruffly.

Primrose sniffled, tears seeped unbidden from her eyes. "I s'ppose," she muttered thickly.

He chuckled. "You are one of the strongest females I have ever come across, and here you weep. Tell me, mermaid, are your tears for the people, or simply for yourself?"

She smacked his chest, which only served to make him snort aloud. "You're beastly!" she cried, turning on her side, hissing as the movement stretched the skin taut over her swollen rear end.

"I'll be forced to show you how beastly I can be if you don't go to sleep," he threatened, patting her bottom. She squealed but smiled into the dark as he bent over and scooped up her hair to kiss the back of her neck. "All will be well, so long as you and I reach an understanding. We need to be united, only then will you see how much better life can be together. At least promise to try, Primrose."

As the silence stretched, he despaired of their marriage ever working. "Yes, all right, I'll try," a small muffled voice finally agreed.

Jago slept better that night than he had in weeks, even plagued by his swollen, aching affliction.

For two days Primrose lay abed recovering, then the following morn she awoke with a start. Her backside chafed against the mattress but as she shifted to ease the ache, she realised that she was tied in place, flat upon her back. She lifted her head and looked about her; there was no sign of Jago. She pulled fruitlessly at her bonds, which had her arms stretched wide straight out from her shoulders, her wrists secured to either side of the bed. She attempted to kick only to discover her legs were also tied, splayed, anchored to the sides of the bed. Just as she took a deep breath in order to yell for her husband, the door opened and he entered, jauntily whistling a sea shanty. He was completely nude and dripping wet. He grinned at the sight of his wife's furious countenance glaring up at him from the pillows. "Jago!" she screeched, enraged.

He shook himself; droplets of freezing sea water cascaded all over her naked body making her squeal. He grabbed a clean linen cloth and dried himself roughly, all the while his gaze raked over her nubile form so openly displayed before him. His organs were finally returned to their normal size, mainly due to the regular dips he took in the cold sea.

"It occurred to me that the only way to keep you out of trouble was to follow the advice of a well-used homily. Perhaps you've heard the old adage, *'keep 'em bare foot and pregnant?'*"

Primrose stilled at his words. "I-I don't understand," she stuttered.

Jago planted his knee on the side of the bed. He trailed a finger from her bee-stung bottom lip down over her chin and throat, between her breasts, over her concave stomach, there he swirled his finger into her belly button before his digit continued the journey down to her luxurious muff, stopping just short of her Venus mound.

"Oh but I think you do. Today I intend to fill you with my seed and keep you on your back so it bears fruit. Hopefully from today, your belly will be filled with my child." His finger continued its slow journey up and around her silken muff, finally dipping into her cleft. She moaned. He lifted his finger from the heat inside her body and held it up in front of her face. "You like the idea as much as I." Her eyes widened at the sight of her slick fluid coating his finger, yet she refuted the evidence of her own arousal with vehement denial. It was quite obvious to Jago from her flushed face and dilated eyes that his wife was excited by his suggestion. "I am so glad you agree with my tactics." He leered. She glared up at him but he gave her no time to think further.

Lying beside her, he caressed and tormented her breasts until her nipples were so taut she begged him to taste the turgid peaks.

Nibbling one, he made her mindless with sensation while his hand caressed her other. His thumb passed back and forth over her full bottom lip, finally pushing into her mouth, whereupon he pumped it gently in and out. Then he straddled her waist. Leaning down, he kissed her mouth, alternating between her lips and budded nipples until the sounds she made were nothing less than mindless passion. His cockstand reared between them and he lifted himself high, his hips centered over her face, his shaft nudging at her lips. "Open for me, Primrose," he commanded. She obeyed, and as he slid inside the warm ingress of her mouth, he gave a long drawn out sigh of pleasure.

He needed to give no further command, she suckled fiercely, taking him into the far reaches of her mouth and throat, relishing the salacious power she wielded over him, one that caused him to moan her name as though writhing in mortal pain.

Enough, otherwise he would spill in her mouth, which would defeat his determination to impregnate her. He lifted his hips away, breaking the suction, whereupon she frantically increased the pressure about his shaft. He withdrew and as he lay atop her he saw her disappointment writ clear upon her carnally brazen face. The minx! She'd deliberately planned to make him spend in her mouth to foil his plan. He tapped her nose and winked. Grinning down at her, he bent and kissed that bee-stung lip of hers that drew his mouth like a magnet. Her face changed as he slid down between her lewdly anchored legs. She mewed with frustration, unable to close her thighs against his invasion despite discerning his intention. He reared his head, winking again. Lowering his head, he burrowed betwixt her thighs. Soon his tongue was darting between the swollen folds of her slick cleft. The roiling of her hips, combined with her guttural moans, told him all he needed to know as he feasted upon her sex. Two fingers plunged with slow determination as his tongue tormented her raised nubbin, nibbling until she spent sweetly against his roving mouth.

His manhood now ached painfully, needing release. Sliding up her length, he entered her with one swift movement then slowly withdrew. Pushing in deep and withdrawing indolently, he enjoyed the sensation of her channel's attempt to hold on to his shaft as she rippled about him, edging towards another spend. He kept his gaze centered upon hers as he took her, never once blinking as he spoke with his eyes through the window of her soul. Her culmination, when it came, brought tears to his eyes. Her abandon was a beautiful thing to behold as she arched within his arms, her golden mane spinning a halo about her ecstatically tormented face as she cried his name.

All day he seduced and coddled her, feeding her from his own plate when she became hungry, holding his goblet to her lips, enabling her to drink when thirsty. He helped her to use the chamber pot when her arms and legs were too stiff from being bound. Afterwards he rubbed her limbs to aid her circulation, then relented, leaving her unbound. She put up no resistance to his continued ravishing; indeed, she enticed him back into bed as soon as her basic needs were met.

By eventide they both lay replete, satiated, too tired to move, think, or even talk. They fell into an exhausted sleep, woven in one another's embrace without waking until sunrise the following day.

When she awoke snuggled in Jago's arms, her long fair hair trapped beneath his body, effectively imprisoning her in the same position until the dawn, Primrose felt safe, with no desire to be anywhere else. Dozing contentedly, she lay still until Jago awoke a half hour later. He took her with a sweetness that moved her heart and soul. There was no uncertainty, she had fallen in love with her husband.

This was a revelation for Primrose. Up until now, her life had revolved entirely around herself and her own needs. She loved her parents as providers, but not for themselves as individuals. In fact, it had only been since their recent visit that she had taken any notice of them as a couple in their own right and not simply as her parents. The concept of worrying about another human being, especially Jago—a man who had no intention of keeping himself safe simply to please her—was unsettling to say the least, and she floundered with the overwhelming concept of a love which now swamped her senses.

~

IT WAS A PERFECT DAY. The sun shone brightly and blue sky joined with the sea's horizon in a haze of undulating, sapphire shimmer. The gentlemen rode first thing, but Guy detached himself from the group to reconnoitre the coast line. He took in the various inlets and bays, quickly assessing which were camouflaged from the cliff top and therefore most likely to give cover to smugglers. His instructions to apprehend the leader of the smugglers was secondary to catching the leader of the wreckers. His superiors assumed the culprit to be one and the same, but Guy French was not so sure of their supposition; to his mind, the two crimes lay in very different categories. His gut told him he was looking for two men but either way, he knew to tread cautiously when lives were at stake.

The ladies meanwhile took full advantage of their married state, enjoying breaking their fast lolling comfortably abed. They lazed languidly until late morning, relishing the comfort of a feather mattress, a luxury after the torment of sleeping upon cheap, horse-hair mattresses for the past ten days. Harassed maids and footmen ran hither and thither, carrying copper tubs and steaming pitchers of water as each lady simultaneously rang for a bath to be prepared.

The rest of the staff, those not involved with kitchen duties, were busy carrying tables, chairs, rugs and cushions out to the small folly, situated on the far edge of the grounds overlooking the glittering sea.

When the ladies' husbands arrived back from their gallop, they too enjoyed a bath, which meant yet more water needing to be heated and carried up through the house. Finally, an elegant group gathered to walk sedately through the gardens to the grounds where their picnic luncheon awaited them. The gentlemen gathered about the stirrup cup while the ladies lounged on chairs as their gossip turned into mild bickering.

"Where is 'The Perfect Primrose' then?" Claudia asked, gazing about her feet as though Primrose would suddenly crawl out from beneath the rug.

"Really, Claudia, you must learn to curb your tongue!" Margaret reproached.

"*Me,* curb my tongue? *Well,* I call that rich coming from *you,* my Lady Wiggington!" Claudia crowed.

Rose *tsked* crossly. "Land's sakes, you two, d'you actually want to spend the entire visit unable to sit down? Both of you hush!"

All the ladies swung to stare anxiously across at their husbands, who stood gathered about the drinks trolley. At that very same moment, they turned en masse to glance back at their wives. "Oh dear, now look at what you have done!" Imogene squeaked nervously.

"Laugh and wave back at them!" Rose instructed. She lifted her hand in salutation and giggled loudly. The other women followed suit.

"Have they settled, or are they coming over here?" Imogene asked anxiously.

"Yes, here they come. Hide, Immy!" Claudia teased.

The ladies shook with mirth as Imogene predictably leapt to her feet. Margaret caught her friend's arm. "Sit down, you silly goose, they are not come! Honestly, Immy, you make such a drama out of chastisement and yet you have confessed that you enjoy it when Charles takes you in hand!" she castigated.

"Yes, and I am sure you fool him least of all!" Rose added with a twinkle.

Imogene expelled her breath, subsiding in her chair. "I am a mother and therefore a matron. I do not like my husband to feel disappointed by my behaviour!" she insisted indignantly.

The other ladies fell into a fit of the giggles at her pomposity; really Imogene was a joy to tease because she always rose to their bait. They were so engrossed in their conversation that they failed to notice Primrose approaching them, escorted by her handsome new husband.

CHAPTER 13

Primrose's approach to the group of women she once regarded as enemies was made with mixed feelings. These females understood love; they were each happily married, they were friends with one another and they cared about each other. Primrose had never experienced that kind of closeness with a woman before, she wanted what they had and she wanted them to like her.

As Primrose neared the group which contained Claudia French, her friends and family, her legs felt like jelly and her stomach knotted with tension. Would they snub or reject her or, worse still, ridicule her? She stood and waited for someone to notice their arrival.

Imogene, ever the peacemaker, spoke first. "Please, do join us," she invited.

Primrose sat in a cane chair next to Claudia. Introductions were made but then Jago turned away to join the gentlemen. She watched him leave with misgiving but decided to take the bull by the horns and speak first with her nemesis. "I don't believe we have met since your marriage. I do hope the difficulties I heard came about between the two of you are now resolved?" She had meant the sentence to sound sympathetic but saw Claudia bristle and realised too late that she had sounded anything but. She tried again. "I mean to say, have you both come to an understanding?"

Claudia glared at her. "Not that it is any of your business, Mistress Poldrunne, but I am very happy with *my* husband. Colonel French and I have a son. I hear Timothy Ponsomby jilted you. I cannot say I was surprised. May I ask if it is true that it was due to an indiscretion on your part?"

There were several indrawn breaths. Imogene smacked her sister-in-law's arm sharply with her fan. "Claudia!" she rebuked.

Primrose stood. "I shall fetch some lemonade," she told them stiffly as she moved away toward the gentlemen and the refreshment table. That had not gone well.

Immediately Imogene rose to her feet. "I think I shall join you, my dear. I have a thirst that only Lady Trewithe's cook with her freshly made lemonade can quench!" She cast Claudia a dark look and followed Primrose across the lawn.

"I need to visit the retiring room," Margaret hissed to Rose.

"Shall I accompany you?" Rose asked. "Claudia, do you wish to join us?"

Claudia shook her head. "No, I shall remain here." She scowled at Rose. Honestly, did none of them see Primrose for the viper that she was? When she glanced across the lawns she was annoyed to see Primrose returning alone. Imogene was nowhere to be seen.

Primrose sat back down in her previously vacated seat. She took a deep breath and bravely began the conversation again. "I was not indiscreet. I was, in fact, kidnapped by smugglers and—"

She was rudely interrupted by Claudia's vocal, sarcastic laughter. "There is no one to hear you now except me, Primrose, and remember, I know you of old. You cannot pull the wool over my eyes for I know you to be nought but a conniving, socially climbing strumpet!"

Primrose didn't hesitate; she didn't even contemplate her actions. She simply threw her lemonade straight into the other woman's sneering face. Claudia's expression of shocked surprise was hilarious. Primrose burst into a raucous chuckle, which continued until Claudia picked up the remains of her creamed, jam scone and thrust it forcefully into Primrose's gaping, laughing mouth. There followed an unseemly, indelicate food fight which soon degenerated into a hair pulling, face slapping, screaming match between the two girls.

Sir Thomas was the first to realise that something was amiss, and he alerted Benedict.

"Dear Lord, not again!" mumbled his friend.

"Ha, but 'taint our wives a-tangling this time old chap, 'tis the Colonel's problem to solve for once!" Jago turned to see what the other gentlemen were gawping at and he blinked in surprise. Primrose appeared to be fighting with the red-headed lady. As he watched, the two women dropped onto the grass. Stranded by their oversized hoops they rolled from side to side, yanking at one another's hair while screaming ribald insults at one another. Colonel French was already hastening in their direction, his long legged strides eating up the distance.

Jago concluded that the titian haired combatant must be the man's wife. "Damn," he muttered. Setting off at a run, he soon caught up with the Colonel, "Any idea what this could be about?" he asked.

The Colonel nodded sagely. "Oh yes," he replied darkly.

"Rose, Immy, come quickly, you need to see this!" Margaret waved her friends over to the open French doors where the three friends grouped together, watching as the drama unfolded. "Good gracious, I seem to be suffering complete déjà-vu!" she declared, fanning herself vigorously.

Rose chuckled. "Did we look as ridiculous as that when we fought, do you think?" she asked, giggling at the sight of the two women floored by their wide hoops and plentiful petticoats. They listed back and forth, their tiny slippered feet kicking and waving incongruously in the air as they each tore frantically at one another's elaborate coiffures.

"Uh-oh. Trouble ahead," Imogene declared, pointing. The three women watched as Guy and Jago arrived swiftly upon the scene. The two men endeavoured to separate the furious young women, who continued to launch themselves at one another despite being held apart by strong armed husbands who soon lost patience with their wives. Turning them over they swiped at their derrieres, the impact negligible due to their over padded behinds. The Colonel began to haul Claudia back toward the house. The gaping friends hastily melted into the shadows as they passed. Jago turned in the opposite direction and dragged Primrose into the sanctuary of the trees.

"What the devil was that all about?" he growled as soon as he'd released her wrist.

"She started it!" Primrose screeched.

"Started what?" he asked, reaching out to brush the grass and leaves from his wife's elaborate dress. "I thought I told you not to wear these ridiculous hoops!" he complained as he brushed around her enormously exaggerated hips.

"I *have* to wear them on social occasions like today. I will not be perceived as some provincial nincompoop! *Stop slapping me about*!" she snapped.

Jago stilled, eyes narrowed. "I am not *'slapping you about.'* I am brushing debris off your person, but I think perhaps a few slaps might not go amiss in order to remind you of your manners!" So saying, he took a firm hold of his wife and dragged her over to a felled tree, thrusting her shrieking form over the thick log. Her hoop bounced high but this time he was ready for the damned thing, keeping his head well out of range of the contraption as he scooped up the heavy material of her skirts and pushed them over her back. The weight of them immediately toppled her further over the tree. Jago quickly placed his arm about her waist to secure her whilst bringing his hand down upon her exposed bottom with a hearty smack. She kicked back, he instantly slapped her thighs. "Enough!" he chided, out of patience with her.

Primrose whimpered, she was still so sore from his rope thrashing that this hand spanking hurt more than she'd anticipated. The heat built in her tender flesh as he repetitively smacked first one bouncing cheek and then the other. On and on, he tormented her scalding rear until she was fiery red and hot to the touch.

He kept her in place when he'd finished chastising her, asking again what had caused the fight between her and Mistress French. A tearful, garbled explanation followed. This appeared to entail some back story of a diary, a deception and a ball, all of which only served to confuse him further. He uprighted her and pulled her into his arms to comfort her. Finally she calmed and, after a bout of hiccups, was able to explain to him what had occurred.

Jago was not impressed with her past nor present behaviour but reasoned that he himself had allowed his temper to get the better of him with his uncle only a couple of days previous. He could hardly take the high moral ground over Primrose's small scrap. However, he reasoned that gentlemen fought, but well bred ladies of society? No, not acceptable! He rebuked her as he dried her tears and righted her dress, smoothing her hair as best he could.

They decided that Primrose should ask Aunt Verity if she could use her chamber to clean herself up before rejoining the company. Jago warned her that another fracas would result in her receiving a taste of the strap on their return to Poldrunne Manor. This was something she wished to avoid at all costs, since her already tenderised rump ached and stung like she'd sat upon the coals of hell!

Verity Trewithe granted Primrose leave to use her boudoir. She slipped inside the house and up the stairs, encountering nobody. Most of the household staff remained outside, attending to the guests' needs. As she made her way along the upstairs landing, Primrose heard the sound of a woman sobbing, overlaid by the low rumble of a male voice. She drew near the sound of voices, identifying the chamber from whence the conversation came. She pressed her ear against the door in order to eavesdrop.

"You knew that my presence here was sensitive and was to be kept understated! Yet what do you do? At the very first opportunity, you draw attention to yourself in a singularly vulgar manner. Brawling, Claudia, I cannot countenance it! How am I to fulfil my purpose here to capture wreckers and smugglers if you make our position with our hosts untenable? Just what is it about Primrose Latimer, I mean Poldrunne, which makes you behave so irrationally?"

Panic fluttered in Primrose's chest. She recognised Colonel French's reproachful voice and he'd definitely stated that he was here to flush out smugglers. She must warn Jago! Just as she was about to rush off, Claudia began talking. Primrose remained fixed in place, listening to her nemesis give an explanation for their fight. As she listened to Claudia's tearful but truthful account of what had occurred, she felt uncomfortable, for she *had* indeed teased and tormented Claudia in the past. It had been *exactly* as Claudia described the past events to her husband. Unable to listen anymore, she continued on to Lady Trewithe's boudoir, feeling utterly ashamed of herself.

Looking in the mirror, she saw how dishevelled she looked. At once she set about plucking leaves and twigs from her hair. She dressed her tangled tresses as best she could without the help of an experienced maid. She washed her hands and face, then sponged grass stains off her gown. Spying a small jar of rouge, she applied a little dab to her pale cheeks and lips. Finally satisfied that she could do no more to improve herself, she left the room, intending to find her husband and put him on his guard.

CHAPTER 14

The weather blessed them, which meant that all the activities Verity Trewithe had planned were able to proceed without a hitch. Then towards the end of the second week, autumn gales ripped in from the sea, and the ladies found themselves confined to the house. However, by the end of the first week, everyone had relaxed into one another's company—all except for Jago and Primrose, who were constantly alert and wary around the guests lest they gave something away about Jago's illegal activities.

The dance was the main topic of conversation amongst the ladies and it was decided that, although the occasion was not actually labelled a costume ball, their gowns should reflect the harvest theme Lady Trewithe had chosen. Since the weather remained inclement, Verity Trewithe planned a venture up into the attics after luncheon in order for her guests to search among the trunks of clothing stored there for topical items to wear for the dance.

Jago and Primrose were invited to lunch that day. After the meal, while the gentlemen toyed with their cigars and port in the dining room, the ladies climbed the stairs high up into the attics in search of plunder. Chattering excitedly, they spread out inside the huge dusty space of the roof and searched among the clothing of a bygone age.

Primrose inadvertently found herself cornered beside Claudia as she crouched down beside a box of hats. Hesitating, Primrose knelt beside her and reached out to touch an enormous concoction of plaster fruit, made up of apples and blackberries which decorated the wide, green bonnet. "This is perfect for you! I believe the autumn colours would complement your lovely red hair," she offered, shyly but sincerely. Claudia cast her suspicious glance. Primrose took a deep breath and plunged on. "I owe you an apology, Mistress French—Claudia. I am so sorry for all my snide remarks and teasing ways. I was unkind and I know that I hurt you but I regret my actions now. I am truly sorry, please do forgive me," she spoke from the heart.

As the silence stretched, she thought Claudia wasn't going to reply and made as though to stand. Claudia put out her hand to stay her. "You did hurt me… and Guy at the time. I have been watching you, Primrose, and I do believe you've changed. I accept your apology but should you prove false in this, I swear, I shall never, ever, forgive you, do you understand?"

Primrose nodded and a tentative smile spread across her face, which widened as Claudia returned her smile with a friendly grin. "Thank you," she acknowledged simply, then plucked the hat from Claudia's hand and plonked it down on her new friend's head.

"Perfect," she exclaimed. "Surely there must be a hat in there for me to wear?" She and Claudia began to rummage through the millinery together until they found another bonnet, this one made of straw and decorated with faded blue cornflowers with ears of corn adorning the crown.

Claudia placed it onto Primrose's head. "I cannot believe it, we will mix and match with the perfect theme. Come, let us show the others our finds!" She grabbed Primrose and they wandered hand in hand over to where Margaret and Rose were squabbling over a fan.

Rose looked up as they approached and whatever she was about to say stilled in her throat. Margaret looked astounded but soon found her voice. "My word, are they friends? And all without the aid of a parsnip?" she stated cryptically.

Rose snorted. "Indeed!" The two women fell into a fit of the giggles.

"Beg pardon?" Primrose asked, bewildered.

Claudia wagged her head. "Mad, quite insane the pair, ignore them!"

Imogene joined them. She held an old shawl, boldly embroidered with autumn leaves. "You should explain," she told her sister-in-law.

Rose nodded. "All right," she agreed.

"Ladies, if I might interrupt a moment?" They turned toward their hostess. "I shall have to leave you now, for duty calls, but when you have found what you would like for the ball, please do join the gentlemen in the long gallery, where I have set out a game of carpet bowls to be played before tea is served."

They murmured their assent and all curtsied, waiting until Verity Trewithe was out of earshot before continuing their saucy conversation. "Allow me to begin the tale." Margaret seated herself upon a trunk. "As you know, Rose and I were once sworn enemies. I shall not go over old ground but we fought physically, just as you and Claudia did, Primrose."

"Spanking us wasn't enough for our strict husbands. When we arrived at Merriton Hall, our husbands—"

Rose interrupted. "Gingered us up!" she finished gleefully.

Primrose shook her head, not understanding the phrase. "Beg pardon?"

Margaret stuck her finger in the air. "A ginger root is cut into a finger thus so, with a flange around the top…"

Rose broke in excitedly, "Yes, then your husband places it inside your bottom hole!"

Primrose gasped, she hadn't expected that! "Whatever for?" she demanded.

"The juice of the ginger stings and burns inside the body but does no harm. It is a punishment that can be used in conjunction with a spanking," Margaret told her. Primrose flushed with embarrassment at the lewd tale. "I could not tolerate the heat of the horrid thing and so I went to find Margaret to enlist her help in removing the root," Rose continued. "Margaret helped me and I helped her, but then we had a dilemma. If our husbands found out we had thrown away what was to have been our punishment, we would have most probably been caned…"

"…and that is when I came up with my brilliant idea!" Margaret added. Rose and she grinned at one another.

"Go on," Primrose prompted, intrigued.

"We asked cook to prepare a…"

"Parsnip!" they chorused together, giggling.

"Absolutely right." Margaret grinned.

"However, we then had the embarrassing task of seating the innocent roots into each other's, um…" Rose coughed politely.

"Arses!" Margaret cried crudely.

"We bonded over a parsnip. I mean, we simply had to become friends after all of that!" Rose finished the tale triumphantly.

Everyone laughed, and Primrose chortled with them. For the first time she enjoyed the feeling of genuine camaraderie.

"I think I shall call a meeting of the spanked wives, what do you say?" Margaret glanced about the group.

Primrose gaped. "Th-the what?" she stuttered.

Claudia patted her hand reassuringly as everyone found a place to sit, either on a musty cushion or a wooden chest, like Margaret. Once everyone was comfortably settled, Imogene turned to Primrose. "We are all punished by our husbands at times, some more than others." She nodded at Margaret, then sniffed before continuing. "As you know, although it is commonplace for ladies to be corrected by their husbands, it is something private and rarely spoken of and so…"

Margaret snorted. "Oh for goodness' sake, Immy!" she cried as she swung herself around to face Primrose. "We are all spanked by our husbands and we talk about that, amongst other things that are generally considered taboo for ladies of our ilk to discuss. Would you like to join us?"

Primrose was stunned. She gazed about these highborn women whom she thought she knew, and realised there was more to them than she'd ever appreciated. Taking a deep breath she began to speak, choosing her words carefully. "Thank you, I should like to become a member of your society. I am honoured to be considered as your friend. I have, er, not exactly been deserving of friendship, I know. I promise I shall keep your secrets and I trust you will keep mine."

There was a smattering of applause. "Fine words, my dear, thank you, but the key question here is: have you ever been spanked by that dashingly handsome husband of yours?" Margaret asked with a wink.

Primrose flushed red with embarrassment and, despite her misgivings over admitting such a thing, she slowly nodded an affirmative.

The ladies leaned in, their heads closer. "*And*?" Rose prompted eagerly.

"It hurt!" Primrose squeaked, unable to believe she was actually having this conversation.

More giggles. "Did you experience any other er… side effects from this chastisement?" Margaret pursued.

"Side effects?" Primrose was bewildered.

"Yes, dear, such as an increased desire to bed your husband?" Rose pressed, as Imogene groaned with embarrassment at her sister-in-law's brazen approach. Primrose gazed about the ladies with startled surprise. She hadn't even admitted this desire to herself and yet here was this group of the *haute ton's* finest, most of whom she had known her whole life in some capacity or another, talking about something so wickedly licentious that she hadn't even given the lascivious thoughts room in her mind, let alone openly discussed them!

"Primrose, I see we have shocked you, my dear. You need not reply but I want you to know that we have all felt an increased desire for our husbands after a chastisement, and though I hate to admit it because I am embarrassed, I confirm that I have too," Imogene conceded.

Primrose swallowed and cleared her throat. Feeling compelled by their honesty, she confessed, "Yes, I have experienced that feeling also."

The others all began to talk at once, sharing their experiences, mainly of the journey to Cornwall, but Claudia admitted that the Colonel had strapped her for her part in their fight the other day. Primrose took her hand; she admitted that she too had suffered a similar fate. Each young woman met the other's gaze and something fine passed between the two, one of friendship, of trust, a message that warmed Primrose's lonely heart.

"Excuse me, miladies, but the mistress asks that you join her in the long gallery. The gentlemen are impatient to begin a game of carpet bowls." The arrival of the maid put paid to any more ribald discussion so the ladies filed out of the attic carrying their trophies.

Jago and Primrose left Pencullen shortly after dinner, having declined the invitation to remain for a game of cards, knowing the henting rain could have made the muddy track treacherous to travel on in the dark. The coach lights would be too dim to show up any hazards on the byway.

Primrose rested her head against her husband's shoulder as the carriage swayed along the route to Poldrunne. Jago slid his arm about Primrose to brace her against his chest as the lurching vehicle dipped in and out of pot holes caused by the wet weather. "I have something very important to share with you but this has to remain utterly secret. Would that I didn't need to involve you but I fear that I must," he said.

She shifted to glance up at his set face. "Go on," she encouraged.

"On Saturday, the night of the ball, I shall need to slip away unnoticed. We have a shipment coming in—"

She interrupted, "No, 'tis too dangerous, Jago, you know the Colonel is after smugglers! At least wait until he is returned to Surrey."

He shook his head. "I cannot, my mermaid... *oomph*!" He gasped as she slugged him in the belly.

"Don't be so foolhardy!" she snapped, as panic for his safety welled.

"Oh, Mistress Poldrunne, you are certainly going over my knee tonight," he avowed merrily. She sniggered, recognising his playfulness. "Seriously, though, I have no choice. The delivery is determined by the French and our customers' needs. I have to go, but the ball will keep everyone diverted. Hopefully no one will even notice that I am gone but if they should, tell them I am in the garden taking the air. Such a devious creature as you can surely facilitate something." This time he was ready for her reaction, capturing her raised hand which he used to tug her in close. Lowering his mouth to hers, he kissed her with a passion that left her in no doubt of his ardour. By the time they reached home they were so aroused that as they stumbled inside the house, they tore at one another's clothing in an attempt to disrobe as fast as possible.

Jago lifted her up onto the Jacobean dining table. Once she was seated he pushed between her parted thighs. "*Avynn'ta ow dogluthi?*" he growled in Cornish. Since she didn't understand the dialect, she didn't bother to reply. His actions spoke louder than words as he bunched her petticoats up to her waist, his hand delving sinuously into her heated apex, glorying in the feel of her silken quim. She groaned and rode his invasive fingers. Her hands made short work of his fall and, freeing his solid manhood, she pumped his thick length, running her thumb over the leaking head.

His hands cupped her buttocks, he lifted her upward. His flanks dipped as he impaled her upon his aching shaft. She wrapped her arms about his neck, her head cradled between the crook of his neck and his shoulder. He snapped his hips and his girth moved deeply inside her, creating the wonderful sentient carnality of possession. She cried out and her head dropped back, pins scattering as her blonde tresses bounced free. His hand caught the trailing mass as he cupped her head in his palm. The other hand supported her bottom as he pounded into her yielding flesh.

"Christ, woman, what you do to me!" he muttered.

"You have the same effect on me," she panted. His head dipped forward, claiming her mouth. His tongue matched the deep thrusts of his cock as he took her roughly, without restraint. A keening cry bubbled from deep within her chest, bursting forth as she peaked in a wondrous torrent of pleasure.

His bellow echoed about the room as his hips jerked, filling her with a joyous release of his own. "Good God, I love you, woman!" he growled. She froze. He looked at her set face with some surprise. "Primrose?" he queried.

She gazed up at him, looking unbearably lovely, flushed from their exertions, her gorgeous hair tumbling about her shoulders. Her blue eyes widened with surprise. "You do?" Her bottom lip trembled with emotion.

His gaze softened as he set her down upon the table and drew her into the circle of his arms. "Yes, *keresik,* I love you," he affirmed gently.

"*Keresik?*" she questioned.

"Darling," he replied. "Why do you cry, sweeting?" he crooned huskily as she buried her face into his shoulder and blubbed. He shushed her, holding her close as he palmed her hair downward in a soothing motion.

"I-I love you too," she managed to finally stutter.

He let out an exaggerated sigh of relief. "Well, thank heavens for small mercies; you had me seriously worried there for a moment!"

Her lip quirked in a crooked smile. He cupped her wet cheeks in his palms, wiping her tears away with his thumbs. "I love you, Primrose, I always shall. You thundered into my heart and soul so now I cannot imagine life without you." He rested his forehead against hers.

Primrose lifted her hand to squeeze his. "I cannot imagine living without you either, which is why I beg of you, *please* stop smuggling. *Please,* Jago, do this for the sake of our future children, if not for me," she pleaded desperately.

He remained silent. Primrose held her breath as he nodded slowly. "All right, all right then, but not until after the night of the ball. I have to finish what I started then I promise to walk away."

She squealed with delight and flung her arms about his neck. She must tell Kerra—her spell had finally worked!

That night, snuggled in her husband's arms, she slept until dawn. When Primrose awoke to the warmth of Jago's strong arms wrapped safe about her, she drowsed, lulled by the sound of the sea as the realisation hit her that she no longer cared whether they travelled to London for the season next year. Her aspirations had altered, she wanted to bear Jago's child here in this old house that she had come to love.

"What are you thinking about?" her husband asked with his husky morning voice. She wriggled her haunches back to spoon into the curve of his loins and was rewarded by his strong erection soaring seductively against her buttocks.

"Yesterday, you said something in Cornish. What was it?"

From his earthy chuckle she deducted it had been a ribald remark, yet she still blushed when he whispered into her ear, "Do you want me to fuck you? *Avynn'ta ow dogluthi?*"

Primrose sniggered. "After some thought, I find I am not as inclined to visit London next year. I would so much prefer to remain here and bear your child."

She found herself flipped onto her back as Jago reared over her. "Is that so?" he asked.

"Give me a child, Jago, keep me in bed all day like you did on the ship. Spend today filling me with your seed. Let's make a baby—how does that saying go? *Avynn 't ow...*" she faltered with the unfamiliar language.

Jago immediately finished the phrase for her. When she remained silent, his brow lifted. "Well?" he asked.

Slowly she shifted her legs, spreading them wantonly wide. Jago needed no further incentive. He lowered his head to hers, anticipating her need. She was astonished when he did indeed fulfil her every carnal wish.

CHAPTER 15

Although Verity Trewithe maintained that the evening entertainment was to be no more than a dance, everyone else, including her husband, knew it was a ball. The squally day was spent inside playing cards. Excitement ratcheted as the day drew to a close. The ladies scurried to change into their autumn harvest finery. Maids had been kept up late over the last few nights, busily sewing autumn-themed embellishments onto their ladies' gowns. Imogene's maid cut out all the embroidered autumn leaves from the shawl she had discovered in the attic trunk, then sewed them onto her mistress's peach-coloured ball gown. Each lady was thrilled with her harvest ensemble. As they gathered excitedly in the drawing room they admired one another's outfits. Rose wore a light gown of pale green, she held the large painted briar and berry patterned fan. Margaret's gown was of burnished copper gauze over brown slub silk; her maid had used some of the leaves from Imogene's shawl to decorate her neckline. Claudia wore a rich burgundy gown with a corsage on her shoulder made up of the plaster painted apples and blackberries taken from the old straw bonnet. The gentlemen wore full evening attire, their burnished satin coats of gold, rust and bottle green reflected richly in the candlelight as they moved to greet and compliment their beautiful wives.

Primrose was pleased with her own pale golden ball gown, although as soon as she slipped the gossamer material over her head she recalled Jago's chastisement on the last occasion she'd worn the costly garment. The dress billowed over her large dress hoop and she straightened the front panel of embroidered blue flowers over her breast. The pattern was repeated on the split silk underskirt. Brushing her pale hair until it gleamed, she plaited it with the long string of silk ears of corn and blue cornflowers taken from the rim of the bonnet woven through her plait. She then wound the long rope of decorated hair about the top of her head. The style was easy to apply without the aid of a maid and when she'd finished, her coiffure resembled a plaited corn sheath.

Entering the parlour, she found Jago dressed in his claret velvet dress coat with black frogging worn over black breeches. Instead of looking dull he looked fiercely handsome. The frilled cuffs of his shirt and neck cravat stood starkly white, contrasting against the rich hue of his dress coat, the deep red accentuating his dark Cornish good looks.

He stood as she entered the room, nodding appreciatively. Moving to her side he kissed her. "You look like a queen. This is the one dress that I did not mind you purchasing; whatever the cost, it was worth every penny! I can even forgive the ridiculous hoop. Turn about for I have a gift for you."

Intrigued, she presented him with her back. His hand came over her shoulder, clasping a necklace of pale blue sapphires set in spun gold. Primrose gasped as she reached a finger to touch the large tear drop jewel that nestled above her cleavage. Once the clasp was secured she spun about and threw her arms about his neck, pressing her lips to his. "Thank you, it is gorgeous, I love it!" she exclaimed. He withdrew another package from his coat pocket and handed it to her. Curiously, she unwrapped the soft cloth. Inside lay a pair of matching sapphire earrings. "Oh Jago, these are exquisite, thank you!" She fiddled with them; soon they swung from her earlobes.

"My wedding gift to you," he told her gruffly, touched by her gratitude. "Shall we go, my lady?" He offered her his arm as she tucked her hand into the crook of his elbow. She wished she could relax and simply enjoy a frivolous evening with her husband. Instead she was tense, knowing the risks he planned to undertake that night.

The salty wind was strong; it buffeted their coach, making the carriage sway alarmingly. Primrose became even more anxious about her husband's planned adventure. Surely this was no night to be shipping out to sea? On arrival the rain slanted sideways, the chill gale billowed under her cloak. Their coach was in a slow moving queue of carriages dropping guests off at Pencullen House. When their turn came to disembark, Jago helped her down, keeping his arm protectively about her waist as they fought through the henting squall into the sheltered entrance.

Inside, a multitude of glimmering candles combined with upwards of fifty people gave welcoming warmth to the new arrivals. After being divested of their cloaks they joined the snail trail of chattering guests who waited in line to be announced by Darrent and welcomed by Lord and Lady Trewithe. Once inside the ball room, Primrose immediately spotted Benedict Mortimer across the crowded room. He stood a shoulder height above everyone else, although Charles Haffenden and her own Jago came a close second in loftiness. Claudia gave a cheery wave as they began to weave their way across the congested room. Jago was stopped at least half a dozen times by gentlemen who whispered in his ear. A hand clasp and a nod, then Jago moved on.

"What do they want?" Primrose whispered.

Jago leaned in close to her ear. "Orders, such as baccy, they know there's to be a run tonight."

A chill of unease trickled down her spine. She cast a fearsome glare at the next fellow to stop Jago—the priest who'd married them, no less.

Finally they reached their friends. After the usual bows and curtsies, the ladies admired Primrose's gown. She accepted their compliments with unusual humility, shyly returning the ladies' compliments, admiring the unique autumn adornments added to each of their dresses.

People were halfway through a quadrille. As that finished, the romantic Allemande was announced. The ladies found themselves led out onto the floor by their husbands who intended to participate in this most romantic of all dances. Jago bowed and held out his hand to Primrose, who stared back at him sceptically. "This is a very complicated dance, you know, we could sit this one out."

He raised a sardonic brow. "You do not know the steps?" he enquired.

She flushed crossly. "Of course *I* know the steps!" she snapped. "I was concerned for *you*!"

Silently he clasped her hand, pulling her none too gently onto the floor. As they whirled and dipped with the complicated overhand turnabouts, Primrose realised her smuggler husband was indeed a most proficient dancer. She relaxed, enjoying his prowess as he twirled her about, handing her onward to the next gentleman in line. At the end of the dance, when they were reunited, Jago pulled her up against his chest and hissed in her ear. "Surely by now, you've learned not to underestimate me? Aunt Verity hired a tutor to teach me various accomplishments such as dancing when I was twelve."

As the dance finished, Jago led her away from the floor over to a private spot near the French doors that led into the garden. He stiffened, jerking up onto his toes he stared fixedly out into the darkness of the stormy night.

"Whatever is wrong?" She, too, turned to stare out through the glass.

"Wreckers," he growled.

"What? Where?" she asked as she gazed through the window but could see nought but the black night through the rain spattered glass.

"See the pinpricks of light yonder over the headland? There is no settlement there, 'tis wreckers, you may be sure. I must go!"

She clasped the sleeve of his coat. "Take help. Ask the Colonel and the other gentlemen to go with you, they know how to fight. Please, Jago, don't go alone!"

He kissed her forehead but left swiftly without replying. She watched as his dark head weaved in and out of the chattering throng and disappeared out of the far door, alone.

Glancing about the room, she perceived the Colonel standing with Sir Thomas by the refreshment table, the others in their party chatting, the ladies sipping their lemonade. Pushing her way through the gossiping crowd, apologising as she hastily thrust through the mêlée, she made her way toward the group.

Her arm was caught part way across the room and she found herself waylaid by an agitated Lady Trewithe. "If you spot Darrent, please tell him I am looking for him, Primrose. Half the footmen seem to have gone missing just as supper is about to be announced!"

Primrose nodded absently, pressing on until she made it to the Colonel's side. She tugged on his sleeve, rudely interrupting his conversation. He scowled down at her but before he could offer any rebuke she interjected, "Colonel, my husband has gone to stop wreckers. I fear he may need your aid."

Guy French nodded, wasting no time in niceties he turned to his friends. "Gentlemen, I require your assistance, follow me. Ladies, remain here, and on no account leave this house!"

Each man cast his wife a warning glance before they hurried from the room.

"Smugglers?" Claudia guessed.

Primrose shook her head. "Much worse… wreckers. I have to leave!"

Margaret gripped her wrist. "Wait, where are you going?"

Primrose lifted her chin obstinately. "To help my husband, he is in peril," she declared.

"Then we shall accompany you!" Margaret insisted.

The other women nodded, all except Imogene, who stuttered out an excuse. "It's all right, Immy, best that you stay here, because this will certainly mean real punishment for us—that is, if we all come out of this escapade alive!" Rose excused her sister-in-law.

The ladies followed Primrose out of the ball room through the house, down long passages that led to cloak, boot and storage rooms. At the back of the house, coaches waited in the huge gravelled yard. Before they stepped through the external door into the foul weather, Primrose lifted her skirts and petticoats and untied her hoop. The other women saw the sense of her action, each following suit. Primrose handed out oilskin lined cloaks from the garden room then guided the women with difficulty through the rear entrance, the door buffeted by blustery gusts. They struggled against the force of the tempest to reach the Poldrunne coach. Finding Sam asleep inside the carriage, Primrose urged him outside, ordering him to take them back to Poldrunne.

As they embarked, Rose noticed that Imogene was among them. "I couldn't let you go into danger without me; they do say there is safety in numbers." She didn't sound too certain, but nevertheless they praised her for her fortitude.

"You do understand why you will be punished, Immy?" Margaret asked.

Imogene nodded. "Yes, I understand that we were strictly bidden to stay inside Pencullen House and we've disobeyed."

Margaret nodded. "Yes, but tantamount is the fact we are putting ourselves in peril and Thomas, for one, would never countenance that. Before we go any further, are you absolutely certain that you wish to accompany us?"

Imogene nodded. "I am sure," she replied emphatically.

"So what is our plan?" Claudia asked as they were bumped and buffeted about as the coach rolled on through the stormy night.

"I confess I don't have one but there is a passage that leads down to the beach from inside our house. I think we should use that in order to get quickly onto the shore. I fear the ship in trouble might be the *Mermaid's Tail,*" Primrose said.

Claudia pursed her lips as she and Margaret exchanged glances. "The *Mermaid's Tail,* Primrose?" Claudia queried suspiciously. "Tell us true now, is Jago involved with smuggling?"

Primrose sighed, nodding. "Oh, please don't tell the Colonel, for he is bound to imprison Jago! Tonight was to have been his last escapade. I beg of you, do not betray him!" she pleaded.

There was silence as each lady absorbed the impact of her statement. "Perhaps it needn't come to that," Claudia offered thoughtfully.

"What do you mean?" Primrose asked.

"We-ll, if the ship in distress *is* the *Mermaid's Tail,* then Jago won't be sailing in her tonight, but if it is another ship and *not* his, perhaps we can get there in time to stop him from boarding the *Mermaid's Tail.* You said he'd gone to halt the wreckers—if so, he is more than likely delayed."

"Of course, you are right! There is a chance to save him. Oh, why did this have to happen on his very last voyage?" Primrose moaned.

Rose clasped her hand, giving a squeeze. "Do not give up hope yet, Primrose, whatever happens, we will stand by you."

Primrose's eyes filled with tears of gratitude at Rose's reassurance of their loyalty.

CHAPTER 16

Once inside Poldrunne, the ladies followed Primrose upstairs to her chamber, where they needed very little convincing to strip off their wet, mud bespattered gowns. Primrose hastily raided Jago's trunk for britches and shirts, tossing them out to the ladies who donned the male garments amongst much hilarity. Their ruined dainty slippers were cast aside as Primrose provided them each with more befitting footwear from her own wide selection of boots and shoes.

Down in the cellar, only Imogene baulked at descending through the trapdoor into the floor. "Are there spiders down there?" she asked nervously. "I do so detest spiders," she complained as she gingerly clambered down the steps into the darkness below.

Primrose had the forethought to bring a lit lantern with her but as Imogene was last in line, very little light shone at the end of the single file of women as they made their way through the twists and turns of the dark tunnel. A loud whooshing boom stopped Imogene in her tracks. "What's that!" she cried in alarm.

"*The sea-ee.*" Primrose's voice echoed eerily.

They reached the open cave where the barrels were stored.

Primrose was surprised to see that only a few remained. She surmised that the shifting of the cargo had been what had kept her husband occupied for many a daylight hour. "Ah ha, contraband, how very exciting!" Claudia exclaimed, running her hand over a coopered barrel top.

Primrose ignored her, pressing onward as fast as she could, desperate to get to the shore to find Jago before he could set sail for France.

Finally they came to the stone steps that led down into the cave. Soon the group stood huddled in the cavern entrance, deafened by crashing waves. They looked out to sea where they could see nothing in the darkness save the white of raging surf. Then there came a huge clap of overhead thunder, followed instantly by a flash of lightning which threw the shore into stark relief. The skeleton rigging of a floundering ship was lit, silhouetted white like the bare bones of some mythical ghost ship.

Primrose surged forward into the torrent of pelting rain, only vaguely aware of her friends' screamed shouts of warning as she left them behind. She struggled to walk upon the drenched sand which shifted and sucked at her feet like a quagmire. Heading towards the swollen sea, she became aware of dark figures; she wasn't alone on the beach.

Another flash and she saw men dispersed along the shore line. They appeared to be armed with staves and axes. She moaned with fear, not for herself, her terror was solely for Jago. Jittery now, she edged forward, unsure which way to go. All she could do was wait and watch, hoping none of the wreckers noticed she was not one of them. Another blaze of white light lit up the beach and she kept her head low, her face hidden. She flinched at the scream of rendering wood, followed by the bellowed shouts for help which echoed from men aboard the doomed ship. She sensed rather than saw the forward momentum of the wreckers as they headed into the breaking surf. Primrose remained frozen to the spot, unsure what to do next.

Yelling mingled in with the ferocious noise of the storm. Primrose looked about her for someone she knew, but recognising anyone in the dim light was well nigh impossible. Then a tall, familiar figure ran close by. She recognised Darrent but what on earth was the Trewithes' butler doing here? Primrose followed him as quickly as the raging elements allowed, surmising he was here to help; she would follow his lead. As she reached the point where the waves met the shore she saw dark figures struggling in the swollen sea, making for the beach.

A figure appeared before her, then his silhouette disappeared as the swell hid him from her view. She waded into the pounding surf, hoping to find the poor fellow, fearing the tide would suck him under. She stood in the edge of the churning sea and, buffeted by waves, stared about her, willing the man to resurface. Suddenly she spotted him: an arm flailing out of a huge wave. She launched herself toward him, half swimming, kicking and staggering in the powerful swell. Finally she reached him and grasped his wrist. The seaman gripped her shoulders as he sagged against her side, together they fought against the turbulent waters that seemed to want to pull them to their deaths.

They crawled, coughing and choking, from the boiling sea onto the shore. Primrose took the man's weight as they struggled up the beach toward the safety of the hidden cave. Then suddenly, helping hands lifted them both while familiar voices chided Primrose for running off and leaving them behind. She thanked God the ladies had come with her. They supported the sailor into the cavern, fighting against the ferocity of the howling gale that tore pins from their elaborately dressed hair, causing it to whip about their faces, making it doubly difficult for them to see.

Deep inside the cave, they lowered the sailor onto the dry, sandy floor. "I thank y-you," he gasped out between chattering teeth. "Allow me to introduce myself, Captain Roger Hale of the *Mary-Jane*, at your s-service."

It wasn't until the women began to discuss what they should do next that the captain appeared to notice that they were female. While the discussion raged among them, they failed to notice the gentlemen coming down the stone steps behind them. Their husbands surrounded them with expressions as stormy as the night outside.

"What's this?" Benedict asked rhetorically.

"Claudia!" bellowed Guy.

"I cannot believe it, *Imogene*?" Charles gasped.

Thomas silently grabbed hold of Margaret, holding her tight to his chest while simultaneously giving her a thwack on her backside.

"Please do not be too harsh with the ladies, gentlemen, they have saved my life," Captain Hale begged in a hollow voice from his spot prone on the floor.

The Colonel dropped to the man's side, noticing him for the first time. Jago brought up the rear with a body of Excise men, some carrying burning wooden flares while others ran directly out onto the shore with pistols and sabres drawn. "Where is Primrose?" Jago asked, his gaze frantically searching the cave.

"She was here a moment ago!" Claudia cried, looking about.

Jago felt ice form in the pit of his stomach. Fear like he'd never known before churned in his gut. The chill running through his veins had nothing to do with the henting rain outside. Fear for his wife robbed him of breath as he dashed into the darkness, intent on finding Primrose.

The fighting was eerie, the beach lit frequently by the eye of the overhead storm. The violence as men fought sickened Primrose. She stumbled about on the beach, unable to help the poor souls being cut down as they were washed ashore. Suddenly shouts and flares appeared, and the wreckers turned from the sea to face the Excise men as battle began.

Primrose gathered three sailors clawing out of the raging surf on all fours; she urged them to follow her. Keeping to the far end of the beach, she guided them toward the safety of the hidden cave.

They passed two men engrossed in desperate hand to hand combat, the taller of the two men skewered his opponent at the very moment Primrose passed by. The victor glanced her way as he retrieved his dagger from the body of his dead victim. She looked down at the dead man; he was one of the half-drowned sailors who now littered the beach. Recognising the victor with horror, she saw that he recognised her too. Darrent. He was a wrecker!

She turned to run into the cover of darkness but before she'd gone more than a few steps, she felt him grasp her arm. Yanking her back he dragged her along the beach, leaving the sailors she was guiding to safety far behind. When she fell to her knees he dragged her painfully onward. "Please, Darrent, stop!" she cried but the shrieking wind tore her voice away. She thought he hadn't heard her plea. She tried again but this time, he pulled up short.

"Shut up, or I'll kill you!" he snarled.

She tried to break away unsuccessfully. "But why, Darrent, why are you doing this?"

He shook her to stop her struggling. "My father, he were a wrecker. I had no intention of becoming like him. My mother put me into service at the big house to keep me from my father's fate. I been there ever since, finally working my way up to butler. Then one day, the mines closed, people I loved were starved, dying all around, excepting us servants, we was protected up at Pencullen. 'Tis no good smuggling, only a few can profit, including that greedy Lord Trewithe—whereas wrecking, now that puts food on the table for the whole area, an' not just a chosen few!"

Horrified, Primrose tried to reason with him but to no avail.

"Come, Mistress Poldrunne, you shall be my good luck charm out of here an' none shall be any the wiser. Good ole Darrent will be back at the house before dawn. I'll even help with the search for your body."

Her blood froze. "For my… my body?"

He gave a cheerless bark. "You didn't think I'd let you live, did you? Noo, you know too much, you an' your nosy ways, poking about in cellars an' such. From the very beginning you were too curious; don't you know that curiosity killed the cat? Well, nasty little feline with your sharp little claws, I shall just have to drown you, nasty kitty cat."

"You don't like me and I assure you the feeling is mutual, Darrent!" She stomped on his foot hard, attempting to break free, but he kept a tight hold of her with a relentless grip on her wrist. His arm swung as he backhanded her across the face. The blow stunned, weakening her, so that he dragged her easily onward, away from the safety of the secret cave over to the opposite corner of the beach. With her own life at stake the battle on the beach receded from her consciousness as she tried to gather her befuddled wits.

A shouted challenge awoke her to the noise and violence of her surroundings. "Darrent!" came the bellow as a man stepped into their path. She recognised Colonel French, sword drawn, his mouth a snarl. "Let the lady go!"

Darrent's response was to yank her back against his front, his dagger held across her throat. "One move and she dies."

Guy appeared to be trying to stare him down until Primrose felt the sting as the blade caught at the skin of her throat, nicking her tender flesh. A warm trickle of blood seeped down her neck and she trembled, wondering if this was to be her last moment.

"Throw your blade aside, Colonel!" Darrent demanded.

Guy obeyed, holding his arms wide, displaying his open, weapon-less palms. He stood aside, giving them a wide berth. Darrent lowered his dagger and loosened his grip on Primrose, who teetered forward with relief.

There was a sudden movement from behind and she spun in time to see Darrent tilt slowly. Crumpling to his knees, he fell face downward in the sand. Jago stood behind him, his sword buried deep in the butler's side.

She ran to him. He caught her in a fierce embrace, holding her tight as she sobbed her fear and relief into his protective familiar warmth. "Hush, *melder,* hush. You are safe, I have you, *kara,* I have you..."

His crooning interrupted by a shout from Guy. "Get her to safety, Poldrunne, while I finish what needs to be done here!" As they moved, Guy caught Jago's arm. "Find my wife, keep her safe and take her with you!"

Jago nodded. "Of course. Good luck!" Pulling his sword free, he ran it lightly through the sand to clean the blade before urging Primrose up the beach toward the cliff, where they moved along the shadowed base until they reached the safety of the cave.

Thankfully they arrived at the entrance without further incident. There was no sign of the others so Jago guided Primrose onwards and upwards until they finally climbed the steps that led to the trapdoor—only to find it barricaded, shut from above. He hammered on the lid.

"Who goes there?" a male voice demanded.

"Poldrunne and wife," he responded wearily.

The door above them lifted and Benedict Mortimer helped them up into the cellar. "Sorry Poldrunne, but we thought it wise to block this entrance and guard it. We are taking shifts; the others are in your parlour. I hope you don't mind that we have purloined your home?" Benedict bolted the hatch behind them.

"Not at all. Are the other ladies safe? The Colonel was worried about Claudia."

Mortimer nodded. "Yes, they are all upstairs. Your wife is quite the hero, rescuing the ship's Captain. He is tucked up in a bed in one of your bedrooms, being nursed by your housekeeper."

Exhaustion washed over Primrose. Her feet felt leaden while her head swam, her chattering teeth prevented her from talking, and all she wanted to do was curl up in bed and sleep. However, when she entered the parlour, the gaggle of ladies crowded around her, exclaiming and questioning.

Jago stared at the incongruous sight of these nonpareils of high society dressed in gentlemen's garb which looked strangely familiar. Hold on, they were wearing *his* clothes! "Care to explain why my togs are being worn by your friends?" he turned to ask Primrose, his eyes narrowing as he noted how pale and ill she looked. He realised at once that she was in deep shock, she needed care immediately. Swooping her up, he pushed through the female throng, taking the stairs two at a time whilst yelling for Kerra.

~

WHEN PRIMROSE next opened her eyes, the sun shone through the tiny diamond window panes, creating a pretty shadowed pattern on the ceiling. She turned her head and saw Jago sat slumped asleep in a chair beside her bed. She reached out her hand and covered his, squeezing his fingers. His eyes opened, focusing on her, and a slow smile split his unshaven face. "You are awake, how do you feel today?"

She returned his smile. "Better, I think, but I am so thirsty."

He stood and stretched, his shoulder muscles popping as he moved to the dresser where a pitcher stood and poured her some milk. "You've suffered a fever these past three days. Not really surprising, you were soaked to the skin and so cold when we put you to bed." He seated himself beside her and lifted her so she rested against his chest as he handed her the milk.

"We?" she asked as she finished her drink.

"Kerra took charge, thank goodness, she seemed to know exactly what to do because I was frantic and would have been useless without her help."

She snuggled against his side and smiled. "You are never useless but I am glad we have her help, she is a trea-sure." She yawned, breaking up her last word.

"Are you hungry?" he asked.

She considered. "I think I could eat a small amount of porridge."

He gently shifted her back down onto the bed before standing and moving to the door. "I shall fetch some and tell Kerra you are awake. You scared the very devil out of me. I love you far too much to lose you, Mistress Poldrunne."

Primrose lay in bed as guilt flooded her. He thought he loved her but it was all false, a hex to make him care; she should come clean and tell him all. She sighed as a tear slid into her hairline, perhaps she should wait awhile. There would be time enough for her confession once she was back on her feet again. In the meantime she would savour this loving version of her husband before he was gone forever.

Primrose was up and about in no time; her youth and natural vitality ensured a full physical recovery. Her turmoil over when she should tell Jago that he'd been cheated into falling in love with her, continued to torment her. She was pleased to hear that Captain Hale had made a full recovery, and thrilled that the Colonel and his men had arrested fifteen wreckers in total. Darrent died later during the night of the storm from his wound but not before confessing his crimes. A total of ten crew members from aboard the grounded merchant ship had been murdered on the beach that dreadful night. Three sailors had also drowned, but the rest of the crew were now accounted for.

She was so concerned with her own dilemma that she gave little thought to her friends. Hearing that they were safe under the protection of their husbands was enough to ease her mind. She finally plucked up enough courage to talk to Jago and confess her trickery. Dressing carefully she awaited his arrival back from Pencullen. He'd promised to be back by lunch time. He had gone to speak with Colonel French, leaving early while she still breakfasted abed. She sat now, awaiting his arrival at table, where Kerra deposited a tureen of potato and leek soup along with a fresh loaf of bread and freshly churned butter.

Finally, he breezed in. Taking both her hands in his, he kissed them. "What was it you wanted most in the entire world?" he asked excitedly.

She shook her head, smiling. How could she state, '*for you to love me*,' when he thought that he already did?

"Really, you have forgotten your dreams of London already? Only a short while ago you insisted you needed to visit London to complete your happiness!"

Primrose gasped. "We are to go to London?" she asked, flummoxed. "How, why?"

"Guy French needs me to return with him to give evidence at a hearing, you too, my love…"

Primrose flew to her feet. "No, no I cannot!"

Jago was in the process of shrugging off his great coat, he turned to her in surprise. "Why ever not?" he asked while shaking the damp garment.

"I-I'm scared," she replied sulkily, chewing her thumbnail as he strode into the passageway, presumably to hang his coat on a peg.

He returned to the room and swung himself into the seat of the carver chair at the top of the table, continuing to talk about the wreckers and the sentences they were like to receive. She remained silent until he suddenly barked, "Primrose, leave that damned thumb alone! In fact, since I still haven't punished you for disobeying me on the night of the storm, I shall incorporate the chewing of that nail into tonight's punishment."

She stared at him, completely shocked. "If I had stayed behind as you'd wished then who would have saved Captain Hale?" she protested.

Jago was sawing the bread into slices and pointed the serrated carving knife at her. "You were very nearly *murdered*, yet you fear giving evidence at a tribunal, one where you will be supported by your husband and our friend, Colonel French? Utter nonsense!"

She glared at him. "Our *friend*? Have you forgot that his mission is to capture you and send you to the gallows?"

His brow furrowed at her tone. "We have reached an agreement. So long as the remainder of the barrels are gone before we leave, Guy has agreed to turn a blind eye to my involvement with smugglers. He thinks that I only stored some brandy for them. He will check our cellar to ascertain there is no more contraband, and allow the authorities to think Darrent was in charge of both illegal activities."

Primrose harrumphed scornfully. "And you believe him?"

Jago pinned her with a dark look, and a tick began to twitch in his lower jaw. "Yes, I believe the Colonel. As he himself pointed out, the only evidence against me is the stored contraband in our cellar, and most Manor houses in England are so stocked, including Pencullen! Fear not, I shall honour my promise to you and hand over the business to my uncle, he has been after me to do just that for this past year. From now on I shall spend my days keeping you safe and amused, my little mermaid!"

She glared at him. "I don't need a nursemaid, thank you very much! I showed you how well I can look after myself the other night!" She began to stir the soup vigorously.

"Oh, really? Had you stayed at Pencullen as you were supposed to that night, you would have run no risks at all. You disobeyed me, Primrose, and you will pay the price for your folly. I waited until you were fully recovered, now it is obvious to me that you are *fighting* fit! I am reliably informed that your friends suffered the consequences for their disobedience. I have decided it is your turn. One slice or two?" he asked conversationally, as though nothing was amiss.

"One. Sometimes I hate you!" she spluttered furiously as she ladled out their soup.

"Ah, domestic bliss. I do so love that nothing changes you, *keresik,* you are still the same sweet mermaid I married." He winked roguishly.

"So long as you are certain this *fully grown* siren won't scratch your eyes out!" Primrose gritted out between clenched teeth as she handed him a bowl of broth.

"She might well try but she'd better be prepared to answer for it." He took his bowl from her with an admonishing click of his tongue.

She shook her head, perhaps the damned hex should stay where it was, at least for the time being.

Jago had been right about the ladies staying at Pencullen, they had indeed paid for their disobedience.

CHAPTER 17

Sir Thomas had thoroughly spanked Margaret as soon as they arrived back on the night of the storm. He'd insisted that she drank the warm milk laced with mead prepared by Cook for the latecomers. Then he'd marched her upstairs, stripped her of the rather odd assortment of garments purloined from Jago's clothing chest, then he'd rubbed her vigorously from head to toe with a linen bath sheet in order to warm rather than dry her. He barely spoke a word above the necessary, turning her over his knee for a spanking that had her begging for release from the very start.

When he finally tucked her into bed onto her back, he growled the order to remain thus until he joined her. Before he climbed into bed he planted both arms either side of her head and lowered his face until they were nose to nose. "You are too precious to me, Bee, and to Octavia, for me to ever consider losing you, and all this comes after you suffered that miscarriage last year. I simply cannot believe that you risked your life after I nearly lost you then! If I have to thrash a message into your backside every night for the rest of our lives in order to keep you safe then believe me, my lady, I will!" He'd pulled her into his arms and refused to let her go the entire night.

Margaret was awoken at dawn with the hard press of her husband's pego as he manoeuvred his impressive length into her welcoming warmth.

Imogene fully expected her chastisement to commence that night but Charles was so beside himself with a mixture of fury and relief that he didn't dare to correct her until morning. Instead she found herself cherished, petted, and loved within an inch of her life as he brought her to several climaxes of epic proportions. Exhausted, she'd slept the night through and awoken with a smile, one which soon dissolved when her eyes fluttered open and instead of her beloved's face lying opposite her, the hated tawse lay positioned carefully upon his empty pillow.

Hurrying to use the chamber pot, her intention was to dress quickly and disappear before Charles returned. She was thwarted miserably, for no sooner had she pulled her nightgown up over her head than he walked in. "Good, I see that you are being sensible. Accepting the justice of your punishment and preparing yourself for it pleases me immensely, my dear. I shall go a little easier on you for your humility. Stand and grab hold of a bedpost. Do not let go until we are finished. I had planned on twenty with the strap but in view of your sweet submission, I shall halve that to ten."

Imogene wasn't about to correct his assumption. Twenty would kill her! She let out her breath with a hiss, ten was bad enough! She wrapped her arms about one of the roundel ends of a bedpost, her body pressed up against the polished wood. "Bottom out!" he instructed. She stuck out her tongue, confident that he couldn't see her, but obeyed, thrusting out her backside as ordered. "Why are you being punished, Immy?"

She rolled her eyes and poked out her tongue again. A sudden slap across her arse caught her off-guard and she squealed.

"I can reinstate the count to twenty," he warned dryly.

"No, no please. I am being punished for disobeying you and deliberately putting myself in danger!" There was no other conversation as the strap cut with precision across the crown of her bottom, leaving a dull red line in its wake. Imogene found it difficult to keep her hands from dropping down to protect her scalding derriere. She tightened her hold on the sturdy bedpost, hugging the thing for all she was worth, eventually sobbing pitiful apologies as her husband grimly continued her chastisement with an even rhythmic cadence until the ten straps were delivered. Her bottom continued to throb with the remembered beat of his retribution, prolonging her punishment.

She clutched the bedpost like a lover until he prised her fingers away and she fell into his arms. He shushed her as she buried her head in his shoulder. "Whatever would Alfred and I do without you, Immy, did you once think of that?" he asked tenderly, cradling the most important person in his life as he thanked the Lord that she was safe.

"I'm so sorry, Charles, I just didn't think," she sobbed.

He cupped her chin. "But you promise you will in future?" His eyes searched hers.

She nodded. "Yes, my Lord," she whispered. He lowered his head to hers, intending to show her just how much she meant to him.

Benedict Mortimer was in a quandary. This was one occasion when he desperately wanted to spank his disobedient, risk-taking wife. She so obviously needed the lesson. He ground his teeth. Rose was unbearably smug; safe in the knowledge that since she was expecting their second child, he would not spank her, at least not whilst she was increasing. He sent Rose straight up to their chamber on their return, to strip her of her wet clothing.

Eloise, her maid, fussed about her charge, pulling a pre-warmed nightgown over her head. She settled Rose upon a stool in front of the fire, handed her a cup of hot milk laced with mead, and gently brushed out her mistress's long golden hair. At her master's knock, she slid discreetly from the room as Benedict appeared in the doorway clutching a small china covered bowl, one which Rose eyed with erudite misgiving. "No, Benedict, *you wouldn't.* I am expecting a child!" she protested vehemently, guessing correctly what lay inside the dish.

"Did you take that into consideration when you put your life and the life of our unborn child at risk?" he demanded. "No, nor did you consider poor little Harrington, who would be left devastated should he lose his adored Mama!" He advanced toward his rapidly retreating wife. She bumped up against the bed as he reached for her, plucking her up into his arms like a doll, which the petite blonde often resembled when her diminutive form stood next to the large Lord whom she'd married.

He sat down upon the bed, placing her gently face down over his large thighs. Her feeble struggles were nothing against his strength. He reached into the bowl set beside him and retrieved the ginger root he had asked Cook to prepare for him. "You should know by now, dearest Rose, never to underestimate me. The fly whisk and ginger figging are good substitutes for a damned good spanking and by gad, my dear, once this baby is born you will receive a humdinger! I am unlike to forget this escapade for many a day to come! In fact I shall mark the days off in my diary until the time finally arrives when I can finally turn your disobedient bottom crimson!"

So saying, he smoothed goose fat over the small, star shaped entrance to her back passage and inserted a long finger, pumping slowly in and out. There was a thrashing of feet and a low moan from under his hand, and he grinned. He knew his wife was embarrassed, probably because she knew that he knew her secret. Rose liked him to play with her most private place, the liquid heat from her cunny proved as much. However, today wasn't about pleasing his wife—quite the opposite, in fact. He reached for the ginger then slowly pumped the root in and out of her anus to get the juices that would punish her naughty bottom flowing, manoeuvring the ginger until it was seated deep in her arse. Then he stood her upright. "You will sleep tonight fully gingered up."

Her eyes widened with shock. "*Land's sakes*, I won't be able to sleep a wink, I shall burn all night long!"

"Oh dear, what a pity," he said dryly as he whipped off her nightgown. "Now into bed with you, and thank your lucky stars I don't use that fly whisk on those pretty, pink tipped breasts of yours!"

Rose hastily complied. As he climbed in beside her he gripped her chin. Lowering his mouth to hers, he gave her a hard, demanding, almost punishing kiss. "You never gave my heart a moment's thought, did you? I would die should anything happen to you, my sweet colonial Rose," he growled. Lowering his head to her breast, his mouth tugged upon a nipple.

Rose sighed with pleasure; her arms stole about her husband's neck as she arched against him.

~

MEANWHILE, Claudia remained behind at Poldrunne. She refused to leave without Guy and so Kerra persuaded her to retire, leading her upstairs to where she had prepared a chamber for her. To Claudia's surprise she'd slept for a while, albeit fitfully. Guy finally returned to Poldrunne at dawn, once the storm had abated and the winds dropped. He shook Claudia awake and told her they were leaving soon. Claudia thanked God he was safe, she hugged his neck when he awoke her. She realised he was livid with her as he curtly removed her arms and instructed her to meet him downstairs in five minutes.

When she joined him in the parlour, she found that Kerra had set them a simple breakfast of warm bread and honey along with a pitcher of fresh milk. They ate in silence, and little was said on the return journey to Pencullen.

Back at the house, Guy closed the door to their chamber; locking it, he pocketed the key. Claudia noted his action with some apprehension. He turned and perused her from across the room. "I made the mistake, when we were first wed, in not spanking you when it was deserved. I do not intend to make the same mistake with you again. I have rarely wanted to punish you, Phoenix, but today I find I can think of nothing else but turning your backside red while hearing you sing your song, begging my forgiveness."

Claudia gasped. This did not sound like Guy at all—what he said sounded exactly like something her brother Charles might say.

"I want you to strip and lie upon the bed, face down. I am going to punish you soundly for your foolhardy disobedience so that should such a situation re-occur, you will think twice before putting yourself into such dreadful danger. Do you understand?"

"Yes Guy, but…"

"NO! No, there will be no excuses. Right now, you will call me Sir. Understood?"

Claudia almost smiled, she felt like standing to attention and saluting. Guy was most definitely in full Colonel mode. Instead of arguing she removed all of her clothes and lay face down upon the bed. She knew she deserved this punishment and she knew he would carry through. What Guy didn't know was that she was thankful for that fact. When she had made Guy promise to never spank her before they were wed, her marriage had almost ended. Guy and she had very nearly spiralled apart forever. She knew better now that she realised she needed her husband to set her firm boundaries, to deliver retribution whenever she broke his rules.

It would hurt, yet she would laugh, she had always laughed when punished. Her brother thought it was some sort of nervous tic. However, eventually she would cry and hopefully be fully forgiven. Only then would she feel cleansed and free, able to start over afresh, happy in the knowledge that her husband loved her enough to care about correcting her. She never wanted to return to those cold days when he would lock her in a room until her tantrum abated. Claudia was full of lively physicality, so spanking calmed her, while the chastisement her husband dealt her kept her linked to Guy by an invisible cord of passion—one that seemed to link their very souls.

As the first blow of his razor strop fell across her fleshy nates, Claudia shrieked with uncontrollable laughter, but it wasn't long before her strict husband made certain that she wept.

CHAPTER 18

Primrose climbed the stairs that evening with a heavy tread and even heavier heart. Before she slept that night, she knew Jago would turn her over his knee. Did she think she deserved his chastisement? Yes. Did she want his punishment? No… and therein lay the rub. Could she submit and accept his justice, or would she fight to maintain her pride? She was still pondering her choices when he entered the chamber. "Take off your nightgown," he ordered sternly. Reluctantly she obeyed and stood naked, arms crossed over her breasts.

"Stop that!" he suddenly roared. She jumped, she hadn't realised she was biting her thumbnail again; the habit simply would not leave her. He seated himself on their bed and pointed at her dressing table. "Pass me your hairbrush, if you please."

She baulked. "Please, Jago, I will come to you willingly but do not use anything on me, *please...*"

He almost gave way, *almost,* but then he recalled the sickening fear he'd suffered as he'd witnessed Darrent pressing his knife against her throat, and his resolve strengthened. "The hairbrush, Primrose," he said again, his voice grim. "Now."

She stamped her foot but noticing his brow lowering ominously, she marched to the dresser and retrieved the heavy wooden brush, thrusting it at him from arm's length. He snagged her wrist and yanked her to him. Parting his thighs, he held her fast. "I have never been as utterly terrified as I was in that moment I saw Darrent hold his dagger to your throat. You will never, I repeat, *never,* put yourself into such danger again. Do you hear me?" He shook her for emphasis.

She nodded glumly. He yanked her face down across his thigh, so that her head and shoulders lay upon the bed.

"This first spanking will be for biting that damn nail down to the quick. I've decided that I shall inspect it daily, and if it is bitten I shall use your hairbrush on your arse until we have broken you of the foul habit."

There was no warm up or preparation, just the appallingly hard repetitive swing of the back of her brush, pounding against her tender bottom cheeks. The excruciating pain built until she was howling for mercy even though she knew her husband well enough by now to know that the pirate within him would grant no reprieve.

She lay still, a blubbering mess, as he manoeuvred himself out from under her and collected something from just outside the chamber door. She lifted her tearstained face to see what he'd fetched. When she espied the thick tarred rope he held in his hand, she immediately rolled from the mattress and scrambled beneath the heavy wooden bed.

"Come out from under there, mermaid! Accept a well-deserved thrashing for putting yourself in extreme danger." He knelt and reached underneath, she instantly tucked her feet up under her body, curled into a ball of misery.

"Primrose, *melder,* I love you. Trust me, I won't harm you but you do need consequences for taking such a huge risk with your life. If I don't teach you to think before you rush headlong into danger then you will more than likely plunge in next time without thinking through the consequences. Show me that you trust me now, come here to me."

She was silent except for the occasional sniffle.

Just as he was about to lower himself to the floor, intending to crawl under and fetch her, a shapely leg stretched forth and he was able to grasp her ankle and tug. "Come along sweeting, out with you!" He tugged her slowly along the oaken floor until she fully emerged. Scooping her up into his arms, he sat on the bedside with her cuddled on his knee. "That's better, good girl, now do as I say and lie on your tummy; let's get this unpleasantness over and done with."

With a despairing sob she rolled from his lap onto her front as instructed. "Push your hands under your belly and leave them there, well out of harm's way."

She did as he asked, then buried her face in the bedding, screaming a muffled cry as the first cut of the rope fell with a resounding thud. Each burning stripe was followed by his gruff voice telling her that he loved her. His words soon had her undone. He thought his feelings were real; he was suffering because she had tricked him with her foolhardy hex. She wanted to admit her trickery but fear of what he would do once he was released from the spell held her silent and miserable. She deserved this punishment, she knew that she was guilty of witchery, a far worse crime than anything he'd accused her of and so yes, she howled. She wept. She did not beg for reprieve but took her chastisement in the knowledge that she deserved every stinging blow.

Jago had felt a sense of masterful justification once he'd begun to punish her but now that it was over and done with, all he wanted to do was claim her, to show her he was her master, her loving protector, her husband for all eternity. When he put that into gently spoken words, she merely sobbed uncontrollably, mumbling incoherently about how he didn't really love her. The only way he could see to remedy her misconception was to show her with his body that he loved, nay, worshiped her.

He held her until the quaking in her body calmed, then kissed her tenderly. His thumbs gently wiped the tears from her temples. She calmed, tentatively responding to his kiss, her emotion fast turning to passion as he captured her breasts and tormented her budding nipples.

Suckling each breast in turn, he savoured the texture of the taut nubbins. Her moans drove him to nibble his way down the plain of her stomach to the cleft between her thighs. Pushing his fingers through her luxuriant muff he tugged her to his mouth, and her legs parted as she gave a guttural sigh, encouraging him to taste her core.

"My but you're wet for me, my love," he growled huskily as his tongue swiped her swollen clitty.

His engorged manhood presaged the pleasure yet to come when he finally slid into the sweet channel that his mouth now devoured. His tongue's attentions coaxed prolific amounts of liquid desire from her leaking womanhood; he knew her arousal would aid his cock's passage during his ingress. His shaft grew heavy with need, weeping in desperation as it throbbed out a command he could no longer ignore: he had to take her.

She was panting and mewling as he slid up the length of her body. Taking her mouth, he plundered with his tongue even as his manhood claimed her. The shudder she gave as he filled her was as satisfying for him as it was for her. He knew that he pleasured her and that she was close to culmination. His hands slid around and under her body, clasping the heated orbs of her buttocks. He scooped up each of her legs in turn, lifting them over his shoulders, gripping her firmly against his hard flank as he snapped his hips, riding her hard, relishing the tiny moans and mewling cries that grew in volume until her song of completion echoed loudly in his ear. Immediately his ecstatic cock spewed forth its joyous celebration, filling her with the physical manifestation of his love.

After a moment of recovery, he whispered his love into her silken hair, mystified by her tiny snort of response.

PRIMROSE LOOKED up from her packing, startled as Jago swept in unannounced. “My uncle is now the master smuggler, and Pasco is captain of the Mermaid! But best of all, my love, they agreed to my price for the lease of my ship and will buy our mules. With your generous dowry we shall be financially secure!” He caught her about the waist and swung her around in a jaunty jig. She laughed and hugged him; the fear of him ending his days hanging from a gibbet could fade from her mind. Her relief was palpable.

“So whenever you are ready we will leave for Pencullen, and stop the night there before leaving with your friends for London on the morrow. Are you packed?”

She gave a sigh of exasperation. “It is so easy for a man. I do not know what to take or what to wear for travelling.”

He looked bemused. “Wear what is comfortable for travelling, and take one good gown for London.”

She rounded on him crossly. “One good gown, whatever does that mean?”

He waved his hand, indicating the many dresses tossed haphazardly about the bed. “Pick one of these.”

She rolled her eyes. “I will probably need at least three morning gowns, three tea dresses, a walking dress, a riding outfit, a ball gown or two and travelling clothes.”

He frowned. “That is plain ridiculous. I was unaware that you owned so many gowns, and where are all these clothes supposed to go? We only have the trunks!”

Primrose plumped down on the bed. “I know, I know but what am I to *do-o*?” she wailed in despair.

“I am certain that you could borrow what is required at the time, and there must be clothing at your parents’ house that you can use if needs be? Now come and take tea with me, then I shall help you pack because we must be on our way before dusk."

It was a riotous caravan of coaches that weaved away from the Pencullen estate the following morning. Goodbyes and thanks were made formally the night before when the guests presented their hosts with a set of silver salts engraved with the Pencullen coat of Arms.

The gentlemen opted to ride, heading up the expedition, while the ladies followed on, travelling within three coaches. The maids and valets fitted in wherever they could squash together in amongst the luggage coaches. It was slow going but by nightfall they had covered more than the average twelve miles a coach could usually travel in a day.

In all, it took them a gruelling thirteen days to cover the two hundred and fifty miles back into southeast England. However, the journey took its toll. All suffered the irritating itch of bites from fleas and bed bugs, which drove the ladies demented so that they constantly bickered. The most fractious of them all was Lady Margaret. Travelling with a smarting sit-upon did nothing to improve her sour nature. She tormented her poor husband to such a degree that Thomas felt it necessary to chastise her most nights. The other couples vied for chambers overlooking the coach yard at every stop, in order to observe the pantomime of Sir Thomas strong-arming his wife out to their carriage in order to gain the privacy required to spank her peevish arse.

None of the women could tolerate her snipping and sniping, all except Primrose. Since she gave back as good as she got, Margaret enjoyed goading her. As their verbal sparring became ever more vitriolic, the insulting remarks became a competition between them that usually ended with the two of them doubled up with mirth, a state of affairs that mystified the other ladies.

It was a frazzled group of women that finally emerged into Surrey. The gentlemen could at least opt to ride to escape the bumpy uncomfortable carriage but their wives were subjected to the daily ordeal of sitting for several hours, constantly jostled, dismally surrounded by their acrimonious companions.

It was a relief, therefore, when the exhausted couples finally arrived at their separate destinations, at last able to part company. Jago and Primrose initially planned to stay with her parents at Caulderstone House in Surrey, before moving on to London for the hearing at the Lloyds Registry. Charles and Imogene's estate, Herstmonceaux House, bordered the Latimers' land, as did Old Heath Farm, where Guy and Claudia lived. Benedict and Rose, along with Sir Thomas and Margaret, lived in Sussex. They chose to break their journey and overnight at Herstmonceaux House before pressing homeward the following day.

On arrival, Primrose found that her mother, Georgina, had thoughtfully given the order for copper tubs to be filled. The couple luxuriated in heated water, soaking away their aches and pains of the arduous journey. They begged off dinner, instead they asked for a light supper of coddled eggs, eaten together before a cheerful fire. Finally tumbling into bed they groaned with pleasure at the comfort a soft feather mattress afforded after the hard horsehair and straw mattresses they'd been forced to frequent in various hostelries.

Jago awoke late the following day. Finding his wife's pillow cold, he knew that she was long gone. He dressed quickly and set off to discover her whereabouts. The dining room revealed Christopher but no sign of Primrose or her mother.

"Come join me, my lad. The ladies have taken the dogs out; I suspect they wanted privacy to talk woman to woman. Tell me how have things been; are you content with my daughter?"

Jago helped himself to kedgeree from the buffet on the sideboard and seated himself opposite his father-in-law. "Aye, we understand each other."

Christopher studied his new son-in-law. He liked what he saw, which was a man comfortable in his own skin and in charge of his destiny. He cleared his throat, feeling awkward about his next question but Georgina had nagged him to ask. "May I ask if there is love between you and my daughter?"

As he chewed, Jago's mouth quirked up at the corner, his eyes tender. "Aye, Latimer, rest assured I love her. Troublesome and contrary she might be but I love the wench, you need have no fears on that score."

Christopher gave fervent thanks for small mercies.

CHAPTER 19

The journey into London took them a couple of days, they overnighted at a tavern en route, leaving early the following morning. It was a sombre ride into the city, with little conversation between them. Both held back fears that somehow this commission of enquiry, as raised by the Board of Trade, would know of Jago's smuggling activities. They silently feared he would be arrested as soon as he disembarked in Leadenhall Lane. Thankfully they entered Lloyds without mishap and were directed to a small ante room at the back of the ground floor, where they were asked to wait.

Colonel French collected Jago, explaining that he would return for Primrose shortly. By the time he returned to fetch her it was nearly an hour later and she was frantic, convinced that Jago had been arrested. Her thumbnail was once again bitten to the quick. She followed Guy, impressively dressed in full regalia, into the large tribunal room.

At a table before her sat three bewigged gentlemen, shuffling papers as they whispered amongst themselves. Not one glanced her way as she walked forward and stood in front of them. A clerk sat at one the end of the table with parchment, quill and ink. An arm slid about her waist as Jago joined her. He pecked her cheek, squeezing her, offering silent reassurance before he dropped his arm and moved to stand a short way behind her. As she waited she glanced about the oak panelled room, noticing high windows set at almost ceiling height. No one could easily spy into this room. Lowering her gaze, she saw a row of men seated upon a bench. She recognised Captain Hale; the Captain tipped his tricorn naval hat as she met his eye. She inclined her head politely. Colonel French had seated himself beside him and the two spoke quietly together. She wondered what was being discussed.

"Good day, Mistress Poldrunne!" a commanding voice boomed, making her jump. The largest of the three gentlemen, who was seated in the middle of the table, spoke. She immediately dipped into a small curtsy.

"Good day, gentlemen," she replied softly.

"I am Lord Radcliff, my dear, you have been called before this commission to help us establish the facts pertaining to the wrecking of the *Mary-Jane*. So far we have heard testimony from Colonel French, Captain Hale, and others about what occurred on that fateful night. However, we are led to understand that you were also there and played a pivotal part in the capture of the leader of the wreckers."

"Yes, sir." Primrose nodded, running her tongue over her dry lips.

"Please tell us what you remember of that night madam; also, please explain how a gentle woman such as yourself should come to be there at all?"

Primrose blushed at the implied criticism; twice she cleared her throat from nerves. "Th-there was a dreadful storm that night. I was dancing together with my husband at his aunt and uncle's house, Pencullen, in Cornwall. We were attending the harvest ball. My husband noticed lights beyond the headland; he guessed at once there were wreckers afoot. He left me to go and try to put out the lights before they could confuse a ship." She stopped, recalling what had made her follow him. She must not lead them to conclude her husband was a smuggler.

"Go on m'dear."

"My aunt-in-law asked me if I had seen her butler, Darrent. Lady Trewithe was agitated because she had a houseful of guests and half of their footmen appeared to be missing, along with her butler. I replied that I had not, however, I became uneasy. Darrent had always seemed somewhat sly to me. He was unfriendly from the first, and a most unhelpful fellow. I really don't know why, but I felt great concern for my husband when Darrent couldn't be found, so I-I followed my husband out into the storm."

The man on the left of Lord Radcliff raised his hand. "Lord Michaels," he stated his name for the benefit of the scribe. "Might I ask what it was that gave you such concern for your husband's safety?"

Primrose considered how best to answer. "I think I would have to say it was purely woman's intuition, my Lord," she replied.

The man pursed his lips and inclined his head, indicating that she should continue.

"I saw people heading toward the bay so I followed them down onto the shore. I saw a ship had washed up onto the rocks. Men were everywhere. I recognised Darrent as he ran past me but then I saw that sailors from the wreck were washing up onto the beach. I spotted a man being bowled over by a huge wave and waded in to help him ashore…"

The other gentleman raised his hand, she faltered to a halt. "Cuthbertson. Might I ask, did this Darrent speak to you when you saw him?"

"N-no, he simply ran by me. I wondered if he was going to help the shipwrecked sailors." Primrose struggled with the constant interruptions. Although she was telling the truth, she deliberately omitted the involvement of her friends. Nor did she wish to mention smuggling, or the secret passageway from the beach into the Poldrunne Manor.

"Pray continue."

"I helped the sailor I had pulled from the sea up the beach into a small cave that I knew existed hid beneath the cliffs, one that would offer him some shelter from the storm. Afterward I returned to see if I could help anyone else to safety—"

Once again she was interrupted. "Very commendable of you, madam."

She pondered for a moment. Had Captain Hale done as the Colonel had requested and kept his own counsel regarding the other ladies? It was imperative that she protect their reputations as she had promised.

"Pray continue, Mistress Poldrunne."

Oh dear, where had she got to in her narrative? Perspiration formed on her upper lip. The chamber felt oppressive, the ticking clock sounding overloud in the quiet room. She began to panic. Then she felt Jago's warm breath stir the hair at the nape of her neck and he whispered into her ear, reminding her to move on to the part where Darrent had caught her and threatened her life.

She continued with her evidence, stopping at the point when Jago had rescued her. She stuttered to a halt after telling of her husband's sword suddenly bringing Darrent down. Then she waited expectantly. Jago slipped an arm about her waist, squeezing her reassuringly. She was glad of his solid presence beside her.

The three gentlemen leaned in together and conversed in low voices. Eventually they leant back in their chairs and Lord Radcliff stared quizzically at her for a long moment.

"Squire Poldrunne," he finally intoned, "we highly commend your lady wife on both her courage and bravery on the night of the wreck. We thank you both for attending this hearing today and giving such concise evidence. We do, however, suggest that from here on in, you keep your lady a safe distance from such unsuitable and distressing events. Ladies are by nature delicate creatures, their sensibilities can be severely damaged by any form of over-taxing. Indeed, it is our duty as gentlemen to protect the fairer sex, sometimes even from themselves," Lord Radcliff pontificated somewhat pompously. "Please escort your wife back to the ante room and return, since there is much more to discuss. Good day to you, Mistress Poldrunne."

All three gentlemen stood, bowed their heads, and waited until Jago had led Primrose from the room before seating themselves once again.

Jago gave her a quick hug after guiding her back inside the small room. Then he spun about, returning to the Commission.

Primrose breathed a huge sigh of relief. Her ordeal was over but why did they wish to speak further with Jago? Had someone informed against him? She gnawed her other thumbnail anxiously, also biting that one down to the quick.

The door finally opened, revealing her husband, who was grinning from ear to ear. She jumped to her feet. "What was the outcome?"

His answer was to pull her into a hard kiss until she pushed him away. "Jago?"

He waved a parchment roll at her. "Oh, this will turn my uncle 'green at the gills!'" he crowed.

"Jago!" she snapped, "tell me, what does it say?"

He hugged her. "You are looking at the new customs officer, Squire Poldrunne!"

She stood open-mouthed. "*Noo,* oh my goodness, how did you manage that?"

His pleasure was palpable. "They offered, I accepted."

She frowned. "But how will you balance that with being a smuggler?" she whispered.

He grinned. "I shall be diligent and hunt down wreckers but I intend to take my cut for looking the other way with those I shall approve smuggling."

She glanced behind her sharply. "Hush, someone might hear! You would abuse your position of trust?" She was shocked.

He tugged one of her ringlets. "You are such a little innocent, mermaid. That is the way of the world, m'dear. Leave the thinking to me, for I have it on higher authority that you will overtax your delicate sensibilities otherwise." She kicked his shin, hard. "*Ow…* ouch! Wait until I have you alone, milady, your mermaid tail shall pay a pretty price!" he avowed, rubbing his leg.

A tap at the door silenced them both, and they breathed a sigh of relief when the Colonel walked in. "I congratulate you, Mistress Poldrunne, on a succinct performance. The Commission has concluded that Darrent was not only head of the wreckers but more than likely responsible for the smuggling as well." He winked at them both. "The men who were captured upon the beach that night will stand trial as wreckers and murderers." He stretched out his hand to Jago. "I'm glad it turned out the way it did. Now I am charged with issuing an invitation to a ball which is to be held at Lord Radcliff's London house tonight. Claudia and I shall be attending. You are both welcome to overnight at the Haffendens' House, where we are staying. It is a huge place with only the three of us there. Charles and Imogene remain in Surrey."

"The three of you?" Primrose queried.

Guy nodded. "My baby son David and his nanny travelled with us. Claudia refused to be parted from him again so soon."

"We would be delighted to take you up on your offer, thank you. Are you leaving now? Jago asked.

"I am. Walk with me. Your coachman can follow my coach to Mayfair."

CHAPTER 20

The Colonel had not exaggerated the size of the London mansion. Claudia seemed genuinely pleased to see Primrose again, and shared her relief that all had gone smoothly for them at the hearing. She took Primrose up to the nursery and, gently scooping the baby from his cradle, she placed David into her friend's arms. Primrose was enchanted by the soft bundle. Small fingers curled in open fists, each tiny translucent nail the size of a large raindrop, while his little rosebud mouth seemed to lift into a smile of contentment even as he slept. She walked about the room, gazing down with wonder into the precious face of a new life, wondering when she would be so blessed with Jago's child.

"Don't fret, your time will surely come," Claudia whispered. Gently taking her son, she placed him back in his crib. "Come, we need to take refreshment and prepare for the ball. Lester will help you dress."

Primrose stopped in her tracks. "Oh, how stupid of me. I have no gown to wear! We thought to return today!"

Claudia smiled reassuringly. "There are quite literally hundreds of ball gowns in this house. Come with me." She led her downstairs and along a corridor to a bedchamber that Primrose discovered had no bed. The walls were lined with armoires on every wall. Claudia flew about the room, flinging doors open to reveal ball gowns of every type of material and fashion.

The women spent far too long trying on gowns, finally deciding on a green organza for Claudia that complemented her titian hair to perfection, and a fairytale dress of soft pink for Primrose, a gown covered in shimmering pink pearls with a shawl neckline. A flustered Lester appeared, explaining that she had been searching high and low for the pair of them. She insisted they go at once and join their husbands for high tea. She remained behind to prepare the gowns and search for matching jewellery to complement their choices.

~

THE BALLROOM WAS A CRUSH. This was almost the last event of the London season so almost everyone in town was in attendance. Primrose adored dancing with her husband. Many ladies cast Jago more than an interested glance and Primrose an envious one, causing her to preen. As their dance ended, the Radcliffs' butler appeared holding a bell which he rang three times. The chimes attracted the chattering crowd's attention as Lord Radcliff himself stepped forward. Footmen arrived, circulating amongst the guests, carrying silver butler trays set with crystal glasses brimming with champagne.

"I have an announcement to make. You are all invited here tonight to share in our family celebrations. As of today, my daughter Caroline has become engaged to the Right Honourable Timothy Ponsomby." Lord Radcliff swept his arm wide to introduce the happy couple as spasmodic applause broke out.

Colonel French leaned toward Jago and Primrose. "I swear to you that I had no idea this was the purpose of the ball!"

Primrose stood frozen to the spot, her hand clutching Jago's arm, her fingers digging in to his flesh with a death grip. Timothy and an extremely lanky dark-haired young woman appeared from behind Lord Radcliff.

"I almost feel sorry for the man," Jago whispered *sotto voce*.

"Why?" Primrose hissed back.

"I look at you, my mermaid, then I look at her. I know whom I'd rather spend the rest of my life with, and you may be sure t'wouldn't be that bean pole over there!" He gave a nod in the direction of the couple, both of whom looked far from happy.

"I have to agree with you there, Poldrunne!" Guy interjected.

Claudia took Primrose's free hand. "Are you all right?" she whispered.

Primrose nodded. A footman stopped in front of them but Jago waved him away. "Damned if I'll drink to Ponsomby's happiness," he growled.

Primrose wholeheartedly agreed. "At least I understand the rather quizzical looks Lord Radcliff cast me today." She sighed.

A toast was made, followed by more polite applause. Lord Radcliff turned, signalling to the musical conductor who immediately brought up his baton. The orchestra struck up and couples moved back onto the floor.

Jago pulled Primrose into line opposite him, ready for the next dance. "Let him see your radiant, beautiful self, show him that you are happy and content. The best revenge when jilted is to be seen to live happily and well."

She smiled into his dark eyes, which reflected his loving concern. "I do not have to play act, for I am all of those things," she assured him.

It was during the second reel when she suddenly found herself partnered with Timothy. "You look very beautiful tonight, Primrose. I regret that your scandalous behaviour forced me to end our association. You do realise that Poldrunne will never have Pencullen."

Primrose bristled, furious. "We don't want Pencullen; we love Poldrunne Manor, thank you very much." Shocking both him and the other dancers, she marched off the floor amidst stares and whispers.

Her arm was caught, halting her before she reached the security of Guy and Claudia, who stood chatting with acquaintances. Timothy had followed her. "Let go of me!" she cried, and he did, but only because Jago appeared behind him, grabbed him by the scruff of his silken pink dress coat, and shook him.

"What the deuce?" Timothy stuttered as Jago strode onward, towing him along in his wake as he skirted the ballroom, heading for open air via some French doors.

Primrose hurried along behind her husband, they were soon followed by the Colonel and Claudia, who'd espied the disturbance from across the room. Primrose arrived at the doors just as Jago threw Timothy outside, taking a menacing step after him.

Guy French stopped his wife. "It would be best if both you ladies stayed inside." He attempted to hold Claudia back.

"Nonsense!" she exclaimed and shoved past him to follow Primrose, who'd slipped outside regardless.

Jago certainly resembled a pirate, one very angry pirate, as he towered over the quailing Timothy.

"I say, Poldrunne old chap, don't you think this is a step too far?"

Jago snatched Timothy up by his lace cravat, pulling him up onto his toes until they were nose to nose. "You owe my lady an apology, arse-wipe!" he growled, letting the smaller man go so suddenly that he stumbled on his dainty, high-heeled shoes.

"I see no reason to ask pardon of a lady who besmirched my good name by behaving like a strumpet!"

Jago moved so fast the next moment became a blur as his fist smashed into Timothy's thin, pointed nose. A red fountain of blood spattered and flowed over his immaculate evening attire.

There was a high-pitched scream as Lady Caroline appeared from nowhere, squealing hysterically.

Jago picked Timothy up off the ground then dragged him

moaning over to where Primrose stood. "Apologise," he reiterated fiercely.

Ponsomby hesitated, whimpering. Then a large form arrived within Primrose's peripheral vision. It was Lord Radcliff. "Do as the man asks, or you can kiss goodbye to my daughter's hand. I'll not have her wed a man who besmirches a brave lady's reputation."

Caroline wailed but her father clamped his hand down securely upon her shoulder.

"I-I apologise," Timothy croaked wetly.

Jago shook him like a rag doll, causing tiny droplets of blood to scatter. Caroline continued to squeal. "You can do better than that, arse-wipe!" Jago demanded harshly.

"I agree," Lord Radcliff added.

"As do I!" the Colonel stated, stepping forward.

Surrounded by men much larger than himself, Timothy glanced from gentleman to gentleman. Resigned, he straightened and turned to Primrose. "Mistress Poldrunne, I am most apologetic for impugning your good name. I apologise whole heartedly."

Jago nodded with satisfaction, grabbed hold of him, then tossed him bodily aside. Turning to Primrose, he took her into his embrace and, lowering his head, he kissed her.

Primrose was vaguely aware of Caroline's continued high-pitched whining as her father ushered everyone else inside, so that when they finally broke apart, they found themselves alone on the terrace.

Jago cuddled her tight against his chest, her head tucked under his chin. "I love you, my mermaid," he told her gruffly as he kissed the top of her head.

Guilt swamped her. "Jago, I have to tell you something that I have put off for far too long."

"What's that, my *Kara*?"

She took a deep breath, the moment bittersweet. "You see, you only think that you love me but in actuality, you do not. I am ashamed to say that I have tricked you—"

He interrupted with a deep chuckle. "What nonsense is this?"

She pulled away in order to lean back and gaze up into his face, feeling tears of remorse filling her eyes. "I-I put a spell on you. I had Kerra make a hex doll to make you fall in love with me." She watched his face, nervous of his reaction, but whatever it was she'd expected, it wasn't him throwing back his head with a roar of mirth. She smacked his chest, furious with him. "This is serious!" she snapped.

"No, no it isn't." He wiped his eyes. "Sweet girl, I've known for weeks about that silly dolly. Kerra came and explained the whole thing to me. I think she was flattered that you thought her capable of such magic but I assure you, she isn't."

Primrose was astounded. "But… but she knew what to do for the hex!"

Jago bent and kissed the tip of her nose. "Foolish girl, she made it all up so that you wouldn't fret over me. I love you not because I am hexed but because you are a beautiful, brave and wonderful woman. One with whom I am lucky enough to spend the rest of my life. That is, if you still want me after I broke Timothy Ponsomby's nose!"

Primrose laughed, giddy with relief. Jago loved her for herself! "I never loved you more than when you dragged him to me and made him apologise," she crooned, leaning seductively against the hard length of him.

His eyes narrowed to glittering slits of wicked desire. "It's obviously time for us to leave. I find I have an itch that only a mermaid can scratch." He spun her about, landing a slap on her padded derriere before ushering her through the grand house. He paused as they met Guy French in the foyer, in order to explain that they were leaving.

As they reached the carriage, he handed her up inside. Once they were fully underway, he leaned forward and lifted her bodily, dumping her unceremoniously across his lap, his black-booted foot resting on the seat in front of him as he supported her. "So, you thought to put a hex on me did you, little mermaid?" he admonished.

"Jago, let me go. Sam will hear!" she hissed as she struggled, desperate to get free but he held her with resolve, continuing to chuckle even as he pulled up her delicate gown and petticoat. He fought to flatten the hoop across her back.

"When we are home again there will be no more of these damnable farafiddles, in fact, I shall burn the lot!" His hand landed with a crack like a pistol shot.

Primrose stiffened. "Whatever will Sam think?" she hissed.

"We'll find out shall we?" He threw back his head. "Sam," he bellowed, "can you hear me?"

"Aye, Master Poldrunne," came the faint but distinctive reply.

Primrose relaxed. "There, I told you so!" She turned and gazed at him smugly.

"Sam?" Jago's keen gaze held her eye.

"Aye, sir?"

"I am about to spank my wife. Keep driving, at least until I tell you otherwise!"

"Aye, whatever you say, sir."

"*Noo…* You *beastly* smuggler!" she shrieked, furiously embarrassed by what he'd done.

His meaty hand landed with a scorching thwack upon her naked behind. For the next twenty minutes or so she was unable to give Sam any thought at all, her whole attention was centered upon her husband's brawny arm as he warmed her rear end with a teasing heat that tingled quite delightfully.

It was only as Jago lifted her up into his arms that she remembered their coachman. She buried her head shamefully into her husband's thick and comforting greatcoat.

"What's amiss, mermaid?" he asked, his eyes tender, amused by her antics.

"You know very well that Sam heard every smack and squeal. Oh, but I am mortified!"

"Well, if you are already mortified, a little more shame won't hurt," he muttered thickly as his hand slid up her naked thigh.

"*No-no,* Jago... *Please*!"

Ignoring her protest, he leaned in and took her mouth, his tongue plunging in even as his finger teased her slippery cleft, caressing her needy button of swollen flesh which always seemed ready for him, never more so than when he'd warmed her bottom.

She lay subdued from the moment he'd cupped her, his finger dancing over her pleasure bud.

She didn't remain quiet for long, soon her keening morphed into a strident song of release.

Her final crescendo of completion caused Sam's brow to furrow, he grinned and shook his head. There was a pause, then came a bang on the coach roof, followed by the order, "You can head back to the Haffenden house now, Sam!"

As he turned the horses about, Sam pondered on the mistress's high-pitched squeals; perhaps t'were a mermaid after all?

THE END

International bestselling author Vanessa Brooks lives in Sussex, England. She has a lifelong love of history, most especially English and American. She has written a few western tales, one notably for the Red Petticoat series, which was such a huge success in America. Her Georgian series, Masterful Husbands, set in the 1700's, also proved highly successful on both sides of the Atlantic

Vanessa's novels are generally historically based; she has a knack of bringing authenticity into the eras in which her novels are set. She carefully researches every time period, and strives to ensure that any historical facts she uses are correct.

More importantly, Vanessa likes writing entertaining books that her readers will enjoy. She includes passion, adventure, romance and domestic discipline – de rigueur within past times.

If you read it and enjoyed it, please leave a review!

Thank you!

Don't miss these exciting titles by Vanessa Brooks and Blushing Books!

Sunny's Safe Haven
Cowboy Caveat
Twin Turmoil

A Shift in Time Series
Lightning Switch, Book 1
Wylde Switch, Book 2

Masterful Husbands Series

His Colonial Rose, Prequel

Sir Thomas's Bride, Book One

Viscount Weston's Bride, Book Two

The Colonel's Bride, Book Three

The Smuggler's Bride, Book Four

Victorian Melodramas Series

Elspeth, Book One

Amanda, Book Two

The Adventures of Linnett Wainwright

His Spoilt Lady, Book One

His Defiant Wife, Book Two

Anthologies

Historical Heroes

Sweet Town Love

12 Naughty Days of Christmas 2016

Connect with Vanessa Brooks:

vanessanovels.wix.com/vanessanovels

vanessanovels@inbox.com

A NOTE FROM THE AUTHOR

I hope you have enjoyed this tale. The Cornish language is a Celtic language related to Breton and Welsh. The phrases and words used in this story are genuine - taken from the Cornish language.

Smuggling and wrecking were popular pastimes in Cornwall, especially in the 18th century when they reached their peak. Many people sought to enhance their lives by collecting goodies from wrecks at a time when poverty was rife in Cornwall due to the closures of tin mines. The coast of the Lizard peninsula is particularly hazardous to shipping and the seaways around it were historically known as the "Graveyard of Ships." However, there is scant evidence that wreckers actually lured ships onto rocks, and any reference to those events within this story are purely fictional, as are the characters in this book.

Lightning Source UK Ltd.
Milton Keynes UK
UKHW011408071119
353072UK00001B/7/P

9 781612 585710